Moon Lake
Angel

YEARLING BOOKS/YOUNG YEARLINGS/YEARLING CLASSICS are designed especially to entertain and enlighten young people. Patricia Reilly Giff, consultant to this series, received the bachelor's degree from Marymount College. She holds the master's degree in history from St. John's University, and a Professional Diploma in Reading from Hofstra University. She was a teacher and reading consultant for many years, and is the author of numerous books for young readers.

For a complete listing of all Yearling titles, write to
Dell Readers Service, P.O. Box 1045,
South Holland, IL 60473.

Moon Lake Angel

A NOVEL BY
VERA CLEAVER

A Yearling Book

Published by
Dell Publishing
a division of
Bantam Doubleday Dell Publishing Group, Inc.
666 Fifth Avenue
New York, New York 10103

ISBN : 0-440-40165-8

Reprinted by arrangement with Lothrop, Lee & Shepard Books,
a division of William Morrow and Company, Inc.

Printed in the United States of America

May 1989

10 9 8 7 6 5 4 3 2 1

CW

Moon Lake
Angel

Chapter one

*T*he old house in the old tranquil town had been home to Kitty Dale for two years running. The house was owned by a couple whose grown sons and daughters came back to it from time to time, but stayed only long enough to get Cook started on one of her "You never" and "We always" sprees.

Cook wasn't her name, it was her occupation. She had lived in the rooms up over the Fords' garage for so long that she almost couldn't remember ever having lived elsewhere. She said she didn't care to remember ever having lived elsewhere; that elsewhere hadn't been very good to her and she'd just as soon forget it. She bossed the Fords when she thought they needed bossing and called them by their first names. They treated her as they would an aging spinster sister.

Cook was not much given to confidences, but on a rainy afternoon when she and Kitty were alone in the kitchen she confessed that her given name was Izetta. "Now don't you go blabbing that," she warned. "I only told it to you because you're going home tomorrow and sometime you might need to write me a letter. Just write Izetta on the envelope and put this address, and I'll answer it as quick as I get back from my family reunion. I sure don't like the idea of having to ride a train all the way to Alabama for such a fool thing, but I got to do it. I promised."

"I don't know what a family reunion is," said Kitty.

"A family reunion is where everybody in a family gets together and fights about things that happened when they were young and frivolous," explained Cook. "I got a sister who would rather fight with me than eat. Her name is Velda Grace."

"I think your name is pretty," said Kitty. She didn't think so at all. She thought that if there had to be such a name it should be given to one of those desert countries on the other side of the world, one of those places where people ride camels and wear mattress covers instead of clothes. "I think the name of Izetta is arty," she said.

"Probably it was my father who gave it to me," said Cook. "He never learned how to live with the bare nubs of anything. If it was fancy, he liked it. If it was plain, he didn't."

"My father is plain," said Kitty. "He's got a black umbrella for when it rains and he lives in a plain house. He's plain. He's why I'm plain too. I'm like him."

Cook took a ham from the oven, put it on a rack to cool, wiped her face with a towel, and sat down at the table with Kitty. "The only way I'm like my father is my teeth. Every day I thank the Lord for my teeth. Food that's gummed is not the same as food that's chewed."

Kitty had only a faint recollection of her father's teeth. "My father has lovely teeth," she said. "Big. White. Shaped like blocks."

"But after my teeth," said Cook, "I quit being like anybody in my family. I've got a picture album and everybody in my family is in it. I'm proud to say I'm not like any of them. One of my brothers howls and barks like a dog every time he hears one, even if it's a block away. He says he does it to let the dog know how awful it sounds and make it shut up. The dog never shuts up. My

3

brother scares me. He'll be at our reunion. Every day I thank the Lord I'm not like him. If I was, I'd try to change myself, only I think I couldn't. We can't unhappen something that has happened."

"No," agreed Kitty, as if she knew all about it. "If we could," she said, "we'd take all of the bad things that have happened to us down to the railroad tracks and let the train run over them three or four times." She was ten years old and didn't know all about anything.

The blue of Cook's eyes darkened. "Oh, sugar, don't let your mind rest on the bad things. Bad things that have happened to us are our enemies. But if your mind gets to worrying about the bad things and you need to tell somebody, you write me a letter. I'll be gone a couple of months because after the reunion I'll have to go and visit each one in the family. But you write me a letter if you feel like you need to, and I'll answer it as soon as I can. There will be somebody coming here every day to feed the cat and make sure the house hasn't walked off, so your letter won't get lost. It will be sent on to me."

Kitty's smile would have made peace with any enemy. "I won't need to write to you. I'll be with my father. He'll talk to me and I'll talk to him."

"Write me the letter anyway," said Cook. "What time did you say your father is coming for you tomorrow morning?"

"He said he'd be here about nine o'clock," responded Kitty. "But it might be a little later than that."

"I don't like it," grieved Cook. "Everybody will be gone by then. You'll be here by yourself. Your father coming here and finding everybody gone but you isn't right. I don't see why he can't get here earlier."

"He can't do it because where he lives is miles and miles from here," said Kitty.

Cook was like a dog with a rag. "I still don't know why you hung up so quick when he called. Or why he didn't leave his number so one of us could call him back. Why does he have to have a private telephone number?"

"I hung up before I thought," said Kitty. "And the reason his number is private is because he does important work for the government. Sometimes he has to do it at home, and he doesn't want people bothering him with phone calls."

"Your father does not work for the government," said Cook. "I wish you'd get it straight. He's a surveyor and works for himself."

"I know that's what he is," said Kitty. She had told so many stories about her father's occupation that she had forgotten his real one. To satisfy the curiosity of the other girls at the Fords' she had put together several versions of her father's employment. He had been a pilot for an airline, then a railroad engineer, then a ship's captain.

Because all involved travel, they accounted for the fact that her father had never visited her.

Avoiding Cook's gaze, Kitty turned and looked out at the Fords' backyard scene—so neat, so familiar, so safe. It was summer and everything was green, June green. Under a dripping bush the Fords' brindle cat crouched and shook water from his gray and yellow head. Cook went to the door and called to him. He only crouched lower and pretended not to hear.

"Nobody is behaving like I want them to," said Cook, giving her argument with Kitty a final lick. The subject of Kitty's father had been hashed and rehashed, so she abandoned it.

The rain went away too, and in their room the Fords looked out at the cleared sky and drew in a tired breath or two. They were Westerners turned Southerners and tomorrow they were going to fly out to Montana for another look, a holiday look, at ranches and snow-crowned mountains—snow-crowned even in summer.

The Fords had the great human ingredients: grown-up heads and child hearts. Their heads were gray, but they still knew how to cut for themselves a little slice of the practical world, and then forget about being practical and romp off to sit with schoolchildren in a circus tent to watch the man on the flying trapeze do his glittering air dance.

This house of the Fords had no bars at its windows and there was no fence around it. The girls who were brought to live for a while in its gaily papered rooms were not criminals. Nor were they wards of the court, minors who had been placed with appointed guardians by order of a judge. They were children living in a home away from home, living in a private house that provided board and room and supervision. Some of the parents of these children were divorced, some were only separated. Of these children there were those who were not wanted, and there were those who could not be cared for in their own homes. When it was summer, those who stayed learned how to plant old-fashioned flowers, to make drop biscuits and beds, and to be thankful for things like food and a free country. When it was not summer, there was public school.

Kitty had seen these persons, all like herself, come and go. Never glad to do either, they blubbered when they came and blubbered when they left. Some had to be dragged from their rooms.

Now the rooms were mostly quiet. All but two were closed because this summer nobody was staying. Pretty little Beth and Kitty were the last ones to leave. Waiting for her parents to come for her, Beth wrote threat words in a composition book and showed them to Kitty.

"Silly girl," said Kitty. "You can't divorce your parents. Nobody can."

Beth lugged her two packed bags out onto the

stair landing, thrust her composition book into one, snapped its locks, and sat on it. She was eight years old. Grinning, she said, "I'm going to divorce them. Both of them. You want to know how?"

Squatted in a corner of the landing, Kitty wagged her fluffy head. "No. I don't want to know anything unless it's something new about me, and there isn't anything. I've heard it all. So have you. I told it to you."

"Tell me about the diamond again," said Beth. "Did your father really say that's what you are? His little diamond?"

Kitty squeezed her hands together. To release something in herself that needed releasing she had made up the story about the diamond. Her father had to work hard to pay her way at the Fords' and didn't have time to think about such silly things. Every month, as faithfully and as punctually as a clock, he gave her mother the money that provided for her, and her mother sent it on to Mr. and Mrs. Ford. Her father was a good provider. No, more than that. When it was Christmas or her birthday and the monthly money came, there were cards from her father with money tucked inside them. He always forgot to sign them, but they brought little typed messages from him saying funny things like, "Don't spend all of this in one place, old lady."

About the money, Cook had said, "You're a

lucky little girl to have such a generous father. But when are you going to loosen up and blow some of the money he sends?"

"I blow it," said Kitty.

"When you blow money you spend it on something you don't actually need," said Cook. "You squander it on some little piece of jewelry or something like that."

"Then I don't blow it," said Kitty. "I'm like my father. I don't blow money." She didn't, either. What she didn't spend on toothpaste and school supplies she put away. She didn't know if her father blew money or if he didn't. Except for his watch she couldn't remember if he owned any jewelry. She thought that if he didn't, she would buy him a little diamond as soon as she got old enough to go out and earn the money for one. Meanwhile, she could be his little living diamond.

Now in the Southern dusk the stairwell was warm and close. To Beth, Kitty said, "I am my father's little diamond, and tomorrow I'm going to go live with him. He needs me."

Beth was silent for a second, but then she said, "You said your father said maybe he isn't your real father. You said he said your father was somebody else and that's what made him get a divorce from your mother."

Kitty moved to set her back against a wall. Along her jawline a muscle jumped and she rubbed it. Before long she said, "They were having a fight when he said that. They used to fight about how the house was dirty and who was going to clean it. That's why they got a divorce. It wasn't me that caused it."

"You said your mother doesn't like you," argued Beth. "But you didn't tell me why. Why doesn't she like you?"

"Oh,". said Kitty, "I don't know. I get in her way. And I'm ugly. And it made her sick to get me born. She near about died. I'm glad she didn't."

Beth leaned forward. "She's ugly, isn't she?"

"No," said Kitty. "Not ugly. Peculiar."

"How is she peculiar?"

"One time she forgot it was Christmas. Did I tell you that?"

"Nobody's mother forgets it's Christmas," stated Beth.

"Ma did," said Kitty. "It was when she was married to Hubert and they had to come and get him."

"Who?" demanded Beth. "Who had to come and get him?"

"It was two men," said Kitty. "They had on white coats and they stuffed Hubert into a white coat and took him away."

"Took him away where?" asked Beth.

Kitty regarded her fingernails. During the past several days she had taken up the habit of biting them and now their tips were gone. It didn't hurt her to think about Hubert or to talk about him. His angel, the one nobody else could see, was with him. In his room at the mental facility, he slept and ate and wrote his poems. Nobody laughed at what he wrote. They didn't tear it up and yell at him to either go out and find another job or pack up his clothes and move out. Hubert knew what made frost and what the wild geese said when they flew over, and he knew how to build a wishing well, but he didn't know much about keeping a job.

Kitty looked at her ragged thumbnail. "They took Hubert to a mental facility," she said. "That's where he is now. Ma got an annulment from him."

"An annulment," said Beth. "An annulment. What's that?"

"It's kind of like a divorce, only better," said Kitty. "It's where the people who have been married aren't married anymore and never have been. Everything goes back to being like it was. Ma doesn't use Hubert's name anymore. Now she uses the one she was born with. Her first one is Bauma."

"Bauma," said Beth. "I don't like it."

"Ma is beautiful," said Kitty. "She's got purple eyes and brown hair."

"I don't like her, either," insisted Beth. "She never comes to see you. She never sends you a present. You don't even know where she lives."

"I know where she lives," murmured Kitty. "She remembered when it was my birthday last time and sent me a pencil box, so I know where she lives."

"A pencil box," said Beth with scorn. "A pencil box. Oh, I hate pencil boxes. And I hate your mother. You ought to hate her. Why don't you?"

It was then that Kitty told Beth what she had told no one. Telling it was like taking a warm, deep bath in a chilly room. Tasting it, fond of it, rebellious in it, she looked away from Beth and said, "I hate her. I hate her good. She tells lies about me and they hurt. Someday I'm going to get a chance to tell things about her that won't be lies and they'll hurt her more."

"Divorce her!" exploded Beth. "That's what you've got to do to her! Divorce her!" She rose and hurled both of her bags down the stairs. They thumped all the way down. She ran after them and into the arms of her mother, who had come for her. The Fords and Cook came scurrying to say their goodbyes.

Kitty went back to her room. She disliked goodbyes and usually managed to avoid the pain of them, but that evening, after supper, there was no escaping.

Wearing her best apron, Cook was the first to come to Kitty's room. "Tomorrow morning we'll all be in a rush to get away from here, so I've come to say my big goodbye now. Do you think we can do it decently?"

"I think we can do it decently," said Kitty.

"We'll help each other do it," said Cook.

"Let's both say it quick so it'll be over quick," said Kitty.

"It's not like you've died," said Cook. "It's not like we won't see each other again."

"No," said Kitty. "I haven't died. And we'll see each other again."

"Your nose is all runny," said Cook. "Your eyes too. Here. Wipe your face on my apron. Lordy me, life is hard sometimes. But I tell you what. Before we both drown, let's decide something. Let's not say goodbye. Let's just say so long."

Kitty blew her nose on a corner of Cook's apron. "You say it first."

"So long," said Cook in a muffled voice.

Weakly Kitty said, "So long." Her goodbye to the Fords was a little easier. When they came to her room they brought a pot of hot chocolate and three mugs. Mrs. Ford poured the chocolate and Mr. Ford passed the mugs around.

The Fords were cheerful and trusting, yet they asked last-minute questions. "Are you absolutely sure your father is expecting you?"

"Absolutely," said Kitty. "When I wrote to my mother and told her you were going away for a while, she wrote to my father and told him. That's why he phoned me. He wants me to come live with him."

"And you have his address?"

"He lives in Cottonville in the same house where he went to live when he and my mother got a divorce. One day right after that I was home by myself, and a letter with his address on it came. I copied it. I've still got it. It's only his phone that has been changed."

"We want you to know," said Mrs. Ford, "that if you have to come back here to us, we'll be here come the last week in August. Make sure you tell your father."

"I'll tell him," said Kitty.

"We want you to know that you have two friends here," said Mr. Ford.

"Three," said Kitty. "Cook is my friend too."

"Forever," said Mr. Ford and laughed, so that the meeting ended almost on a festive note. That night Kitty slept a little better than she had been sleeping.

The next morning at a quarter to eight a taxi came for Cook, and the airport limousine came for the Fords. Mr. Ford had brought all of Kitty's things down to the front hall. He handed Kitty the key to the front door and said to give it to her father when he came. "Tell him to lock up behind you and hang the key on the hook under the steps. He'll see where it is."

Mrs. Ford put her arms around Kitty. "Don't forget us. We love you."

Everybody kissed. The kisses were wet and salty. Cook had on her black Sunday dress and black Sunday shoes.

At the last moment Kitty thought that she would break down and run after the taxi or the limousine screaming, "Take me with you! My father didn't call! I just said that so you could go and have your vacations. Oh, come back! I don't know where I'm supposed to go! Somebody! Take me with you!"

That didn't happen. Kitty pasted a smile on her lips and held her head high. When the street lay empty again, she stooped and picked one of the daisies from a bed she had helped plant. It was pink and had a long stem.

When her taxi came to take her to the bus station, she showed the flower to the driver. He had a sad face and said sure, he liked flowers. "They go with kids," he said. "If I don't know anything else, I know that. I got six little dirt farmers of my own. But where you packing off to, lady?"

"I've been living here for two years, but now I'm going to Cottonville to live with my father," said Kitty. "He needs me."

The taxi driver eyed her luggage, which consisted of one bag and a wicker basket. "You're clearing out of here after two years and this is all you got to take with you?"

"I grew out of some of my clothes," explained Kitty. "So I gave them to Cook to give to somebody smaller than me. My father will buy me all new stuff."

"Little lady," said the driver, "I don't need to know *all* about you, but before we go tearing off to the bus station I need to know that you aren't just fixing to be one of them runaway kids. Isn't there somebody around here I could speak to? Somebody older than you?"

"They've all gone," said Kitty, "and I have to go too. My father couldn't come for me, so I've got to go on the bus."

"You ought to have a note pinned to you," commented the driver. He took the key from Kitty, locked the door, and hung the key on the hook under the step. At the bus station he stood at the ticket counter with her until she had her ticket and her bag had been checked through to Cottonville. He explained to her what the baggage check stub was for and said she could carry the basket onto the bus. It had a lid that closed and contained a snapshot of Hubert, a letter from Hubert, a comb, her money, a pair of pajamas, and wrapped in the pajamas, a gift for her father.

The gift was one of her school achievements. The head of a young girl modeled in clay, it had been fired in the school's kiln. The other students in the project had made plates and animals.

Her project teacher had been impressed, and said, "Remarkable. It's you, isn't it?"

"Yes, but I had to try twice," Kitty had answered. "The first one exploded when I put it in the kiln because I forgot to make a hole in it so it would dry inside. It wasn't dry enough when I put it in the kiln."

"I remember," said the teacher.

"I didn't paint it because I like natural things," Kitty responded.

Now on the way to Cottonville she held the basket on her lap and opened it several times to reach inside to pat the head. Her father would put it on his dresser. No, he'd put it on the table in his living room where the light from a lamp would shine on it. When his friends came he'd show it to them and say, "It's my daughter and she made it. She has been touched by a wand."

Kitty had never ridden on a cross-country bus before, but thought she shouldn't tell this to any of the other passengers. They might think she was one of those runaway kids, might stop the bus and have her put off, or else call the police.

The man in the seat next to hers read a magazine. Occasionally he lowered it and carried on a little whispered conversation with himself. Once he jabbed at a page, turned his head so that his gaze rested on her, and said, "Well, I guess we can't blame that on the horse or the plow or floppy shoelaces, can we?"

Kitty didn't answer. She thought that she shouldn't talk to him because Cook had advised her never to talk to strangers, never to give her real name to one, to say that her name was Wilhelmenia Von Zock if she was asked. "I once knew a girl who claimed that was her name," Cook had said. "It wasn't. Her real name was Mildred Sack. Nobody believed her name was Wilhelmenia Von Zock. They won't believe you either, but you tell it to them anyway. While they're thinking about it you'll have time to get away."

The man in the seat next to Kitty's didn't ask her name. Through low hills the curving highway rose and dipped. When the bus pulled into the Cottonville terminal, Kitty got off, claimed her bag, and went outside. One side of the street was lined with stores. On the other there was a shady park where people sat on benches. The sun was high and hot. From a church somewhere, a bell rang the news of some event.

It's telling about me, thought Kitty. To hold her nervous laugh back she sucked her cheeks. It was silly to think that the bell ringer knew that she had come.

She didn't want to ask strangers for directions to her father's street, but when a big girl pushing a baby carriage came out of the park and smiled at her, she asked and was directed. Imitating the girl, the child in the carriage raised up to point and add his own directions. Both his directions and the girl's were fuzzy and some of the streets were not marked, so it took a while for Kitty to locate first the right street and then the house with the right name on its curbside mailbox.

The street was occupied by only two houses set far apart. In between were empty sandlots grown over with weeds and wild grass. Nothing in the lots moved.

The Dale house had wide front windows that looked out onto the street. Set off to one side there was what appeared to be a utility or storage shed.

Kitty saw that the windows of the house were closed and that the blinds had been drawn to their sills. In the center of the front door there was a doorbell, the button kind. Kitty put her finger on the button and heard the inside chimes—three notes. The door remained closed.

Kitty pushed the button again, and again. After the third try she set her bag and her basket beside the door and went around to the back of the house. Shaded by a porch, its rear door and windows were closed, but the windows were uncovered.

Kitty went from window to window to peer in. There was her father's kitchen, so neat, everything shiny white. At the table there in the center of the room was where her father ate his frozen food suppers and his dry cereal breakfasts. That kind of food was not good for him, and neither was eating alone. After working all day he should come home to the smell of things bubbling on the stove and things browning in the oven. He should have somebody to eat with.

Envisioning the comfort and help she would be to her father, Kitty started around again to the front of the house. On the way she passed the shed. The shed's door was ajar and she went to it. Under her hand it swung open and she looked in at household overflow. On one wall there was a row of coats hanging lopsided from wire hangers. Beneath these was a shelf of old small kitchen appliances and a foot locker with a blanket draped over its top. Set about on the rough wooden floor were lamps, stacks of books and boxes, a radio, a child's table and chair set.

Kitty did not remember ever having owned a table and chair set, and after a moment of indecision went into the shed for a closer look. Kneeling beside the small painted table, she frowned. She could remember herself as a four-year-old. She had had a pair of candy-striped pajamas with feet in them. She could remember herself as a three-year-old, could remember the toy tea set and her father sitting with her on a cold, twosome afternoon to drink cambric tea from the thimble-sized cups. There was an even earlier memory of her father holding his watch to her ear so that she could listen to its magic ticking. But there was no memory of this table and these chairs. They had never been hers.

Kitty rose and left the shed. She hadn't eaten or drunk anything since breakfast. She was too excited to think about hunger, but was so thirsty she thought she could drink a quart of anything. A garden hose lying in the front yard caught her eye and she followed it out to where it was connected to a spigot. The water had the faint taste of sulfur.

Out in the empty lots a young wind was making the high grass blades bend and weave, and through them now there came two small children, a boy and a girl. Thick as two thieves, they had their heads down and were deep in conversation. At the edge of the yard they stopped and looked up. They had spied Kitty.

"Tildy!" cried the little boy. "You're back!" His cheeks were fat and pink and he wore glasses.

"That's not Matilda," said the girl. She wore a pair of Mama shoes. They were green, had high heels and pointed toes, and were sizes too big for her feet. "Brother," she said, "be quiet. That's not Tildy. It's somebody else."

She was trying to hold on to Brother's hand, but he pulled away from her and ran forward to peer at Kitty. "No," he said, "you're not Tildy."

Kitty looked down into Brother's upturned face. "Who is Tildy?"

"Tildy Dale," Brother answered, laughing. "She lives here. Mr. Dale and Mrs. Dale too. This is their house, but they've gone away now. They went to Colorado to see mountains and aren't coming back till Tildy has to go to school again."

Kitty's heart had begun to skip beats. To stop its commotion she put her hand on her chest. The commotion didn't stop. "Did they say where in Colorado, Brother?" she asked. "Did they say the name of the town?"

"It was Colorado," said Brother.

On an intake of breath, Kitty said, "Brother, are you sure?"

Brother stuck his stomach out as far as it would stretch. "Sure I'm sure. I don't tell anything unless it's sure. Sister would hit me if I did."

Still at the edge of the yard, Sister called out, "Brother. Come on. We've got to go."

Brother had a last-minute piece of rush information. "Tildy's adopted. She didn't belong to Mr. Dale before Mr. Dale and Mrs. Dale got married, but now she belongs to both of them."

"Brother!" called Sister.

"I'm coming, I'm coming!" screamed Brother. He whirled and sped away.

Kitty kept her eyes fixed on Sister's green shoes until she could no longer see them. She was thirsty again, and again drank from the garden hose. After she had drunk all she could hold, she felt dizzy, so she turned the water on full force and held her face in its spray. Drops of it wet her shirt and flew up into her hair. On the way back to the bus station most of the wetness dried.

After she had bought her ticket and checked her bag, she carried her basket into the ladies' rest room. A woman at one of the sinks was making her red lips redder. Out of the corner of her eye she watched as Kitty took her comb from her basket and raked her brown hair. Her own hair was black, black. She asked a traveler's question. "You coming or going?"

"Going," answered Kitty.

"To where?" asked the woman.

"To where my mother lives," evaded Kitty and, picking up her basket, she hurried out. She bought a bar of chocolate candy from a vending machine, but she didn't eat it. When she left the bus at Plainfield she left the candy bar in her seat.

Chapter two

At one time the town of Plainfield had been one of those little backwoods places that wanted to grow but didn't know how. Attracted by its natural resources, its good citizens had come with shining ideas.

One by one the ideas lost their shine. They failed because they weren't sound in the first place, because everybody had a different one, and because nobody stood up to shout, "Wait! Wait! We are floundering! What we need is a leader!"

Nobody wanted to be leader because it's easier

to be led than to lead. So after a while the bank closed its doors and the young citizens of the town took up the hobby of serious loafing. The older citizens looked around at the confusion and waste and said, "What now?"

They were still asking that question when one day into their midst came a young Texan named Edwin Johnson. Son of a well-heeled widow, he had been to college and so he knew the difference between an idea and a hole in the ground. He had a sound idea and he put it to work. He put the people to work. He built a brick factory out on Moon Lake Road. He built churches. Under his persuasion the old frame schoolhouse was razed and a new one erected. The bank reopened its doors for business.

The simple, solid citizens of Plainfield cheered. They had their leader.

Kitty's mother lived on Moon Lake Road. An old man on a bicycle told her where to find it. Moon Lake Road was a thoroughfare that twisted toward the south, in and out of country emptiness—though country was only a mile or so removed from town. West of Moon Lake Road, stretching back and back as far as the eye could see, was woodland dense with roots, weeds, and columns of trees.

A lane jutting off from the road led to a house, but not the one that Kitty sought. A roadside sign with a pointing arrow told her that the house was where a person named Aunt Petal lived, and that Aunt Petal performed marriages. Next to the marriage sign was another sign advertising fresh blackberries and blackberry jam for sale. The signs were short, thin boards attached to two posts. The lettering on them was dull white.

Farther south on Moon Lake Road was a cluster of country stores, an ice plant, and the brick factory. On beyond the factory were meadows. Sprawled in one of these was a lake. Except for the sound of a truck zipping along on the road, all was quiet.

It was late in the afternoon before Kitty found the house she was looking for. Structured of red brick, small and severely plain, it was the kind of house that somebody young and in a hurry to be done with it would build. One of its steps had a little hollow in its concrete center.

Mounting the steps, Kitty had the impulse to turn and run, but run to where was the desperate question to which she had no answer. So she set her bag and basket down, raised the knocker, and banged it twice. There was a short wait and then the door opened.

Kitty faced her mother. In her mind a dozen times, a hundred times, she had rehearsed this meeting, schooling herself to stand with her shoulders back and her chin lifted.

The hours of schooling paid off. "Ma," said Kitty. "It's me."

Her mother took an astonished step backward and then two forward. She was wearing a lavender dress with long pleated sleeves and a jeweled belt. Her hair was curled around her face like a girl's. She didn't look like a mother. "Oh," she faltered. "Oh." But then she found a stronger voice. "Well, it really is, isn't it? Where did you come from?"

"From where I've been," replied Kitty, feeling out a brave way. "The Fords had to go away, so I came to stay with you for a while."

"Wonderful," said her mother. She took another step toward Kitty, hesitated, and then leaned to kiss and be kissed. "But why didn't you let me know you were coming?"

Kitty knew the kisses meant nothing. Long ago they had stopped meaning something. Ashamed of them, Kitty drew away. "I didn't have time. I was going to go live with my father, but he's married again and has gone to Colorado to the mountains. He isn't coming back until Tildy has to go to school again."

Her mother blinked. "Tildy?"

"Her name is Matilda," said Kitty. "My father has adopted her and that's all I know."

Her mother said, "Well. Well." She seemed stuck with the word. When she leaned to pick up

Kitty's bag and basket she said it again. "Well, let's get inside where we can talk a little before I have to go."

"Where are you going?" asked Kitty.

"Let's get inside and I'll tell you," said her mother.

Inside, the house was fussy. The floors were carpeted and there were flowered drapes at the living room windows. Beneath the windows was a sectional sofa that had been pulled apart and had tables standing between the sections. The tables were covered with lace cloths made of plastic. On one of them was a bowl of artificial fruit. There were magazines, but no books. A framed photograph of Kitty's mother looked down from a wall.

Her mother hurried Kitty's bag and basket off to another room and came back. She wanted to know how Kitty had come.

"Bus," said Kitty, "and then I walked out to here."

Her mother was at the bowl of fruit, pulling at the grape cluster to make it hang over the bowl's rim. "I've been working in the factory down the road. It makes bricks."

"I saw it," said Kitty. Like a guest, she was sitting on one of the sofa pieces. She wondered if there might be fleas in its upholstery because something was making her itch.

"That's why I've been living here," her mother rattled on. "It's close enough so that I've been able to walk back and forth to my job. I don't have a car."

"You said you were about to go someplace," said Kitty.

Her mother went to a window, drew back a drape, and looked out. "I'm going away with Edwin Johnson. We're going to be married and right after the ceremony we're going to Texas. Edwin's mother lives there."

Kitty thought of giving herself up to acting like a bad child. She was tired. She was hungry and thirsty. She wanted the relief of sleep in a quiet room and not having to think about tomorrow and tomorrow. She wanted Cook and the Fords. More than all, she wanted the luxury of being ten years old. "What about me?" she asked.

Her mother let the drape fall back into place and turned from the window. "That's the problem. What are we going to do about you? I wish I had known you were coming. You should have let me know."

"Maybe I should go to a hotel," said Kitty. "Except I don't think they'd let me in, and doesn't that cost a lot?"

Her mother plunged past that suggestion. "Oh, be quiet. I'm trying to think."

"Who is Edwin Johnson?" Kitty asked.

"He owns the brick factory," answered her mother. "And this house. He's a very prominent man. He's respected and well off. He's young and is going to give me all the things I've never had. He's the only man who has ever truly loved me."

Don't argue with her, Kitty told herself, arguing with herself. If love came up and fell on her she wouldn't know what it was.

Kitty began to argue. "My father loved you. And Hubert. Hubert still does."

Her mother ran a finger around the inside of her belt. "Hubert is dead."

"No, he isn't," said Kitty. "He's still where you had them take him that day. I wrote to him and he wrote back and sent me his picture."

"He is dead to me," retorted her mother. "And from now on he's dead to you too. I don't want you to write to him again."

"Why?" asked Kitty. She was still the uninvited guest and, as always, a troublemaker. Her mother's face said so.

Her mother was touring the room, eyeing its furnishings as if she had never seen them before. Her short hair bounced. She came back to stand before Kitty. "Because I want it that way. Listen. I'm not on a witness stand. I don't have to explain anything to you. But if you must know, Edwin doesn't know about Hubert and I don't want him to."

Again Kitty asked, "Why?"

"Because he's ten years younger than I am!" exploded her mother. "And like everybody else in this town, he's very moral. Everybody here has a lot of old-timey ideas about marriage and divorce. That's the way they are. They're old-fashioned."

"Hubert was sweet," said Kitty.

"I'm telling you like it is," said her mother. "And I want you to pay attention. I don't want Edwin to know anything about Hubert. He's accepted my divorce from your father because he knows how mean your father was to me, but he wouldn't accept an annulment from another husband—especially a crazy."

"Hubert cleaned the house and took your breakfast to you so you wouldn't have to get out of bed to eat it," said Kitty.

"He was sick," said her mother. "And it certainly wasn't my function in life to hang around waiting to see if he was going to get better. Anyway, he never happened. My marriage to him was annulled. It's like it never happened."

Kitty gave herself up to acting like a bad child. She pushed her chin out and put a barb in her voice. "It's like a disease where everybody gets it."

"What is?" said her mother sharply.

"All this marrying and un-marrying. You'd think nobody had anything else to do. Now the preachers have even got signs out on the road telling people where to go if they want to get married."

"What preachers are you talking about?" inquired her mother.

"That one named Aunt Petal down the road. She's got a sign that says marriages performed. You'd think she'd be ashamed to advertise it like that. Like she was running a store or something."

"Aunt Petal is not a preacher," reported her mother. "She's a nobody. She's a notary public and anything else she happens to think of that will make her a dollar. She's a disgrace to Moon Lake Road. So is that hovel of hers she calls her home. She won't sell it and she won't fix it and she won't move. She inherited it from a crackpot she used to work for, and she says she's going to die in it."

"Whose aunt is she?" inquired Kitty.

"Everybody's," replied her mother. "Whether she's related to them or not." A thought raced across her face. She clapped a hand to her forehead. "That's it! Aunt Petal! You can go stay with her while I'm gone. She'll be tickled to earn what I'll pay her."

I am not ten years old, thought Kitty, and I don't have a mother. I am fifty years old and should go live under a tree. Kitty made her face blank and sat with her hands folded while her mother went to the kitchen to use the phone. When she came back she said that the arrangements were all made. Kitty was to go to Aunt Petal's right after supper. She musn't go before then because Aunt Petal needed some time to clear out her spare room. "There's stuff in the refrigerator for your supper," she said. "You can cook, can't you?"

"I can make drop biscuits," said Kitty.

"Wonderful," said her mother, and went into her bedroom to put on a hat and find her handbag. The hat was purple, and because she knew she was expected to, Kitty admired it. "You don't look a bit like a Ma. You look like a bride," she said.

Her mother was at the bowl of fruit. She stood the banana upright. It fell over against the grapes and she buried it under them. "That reminds me," she said. "When Edwin comes he'll have some friends with him. They're going to be our wedding witnesses. When I introduce you, do you think you can remember not to call me Ma?"

Kitty glanced around the room for something fresh to look at, but she had already memorized everything in it. "Sure," she said. "I can do that. I've done it before. Who am I going to be this time? Your cousin or your little sister?"

Her mother started to draw on her gloves, changed her mind, and put them in her handbag. "I told Aunt Petal that you were my cousin and that's what I'd like to tell Edwin's friends." With only a little quiver of guilt showing in her face, she said, "I'm sorry if this doesn't agree with you. I don't like it either, but you've got to understand that I have to live too. You've got to understand that there's the difference between Edwin's age and mine. I wouldn't care if there was a hundred years' difference, but Edwin does. It's embarrassing to him and he doesn't want anyone else to know. He's got a point. Our private lives are our own."

I will not, thought Kitty, lie for this person again. I will not, she thought, pretend for her again. Yet when Edwin and his friends arrived and she was introduced as her mother's cousin she grinned and said, "Hey." And cried, "Doesn't Bauma look pretty, all dressed up for her wedding?"

Edwin had a cherub's face, round and smooth. He looked like a high school football player dressed for Sunday school. He put on an act for his friends. "Well, lookee here!" he yelped. "It's Miss Kitty dropped in to see us off. Now isn't that about the nicest thing you've heard all day?"

The friends said yes, that they hadn't heard anything nicer all day. Indulgently, they looked at Kitty. Edwin looked at her warily. His large clear eyes said that he didn't like her. The expression in them wished for her to melt, to disappear, to do anything but be a part of his new life. Continuing his act, he asked, "How in the world are you?"

"I don't hurt anywhere," said Kitty. This wasn't true. She hurt everywhere, and she was frightened and more than a little angry. The hurt and the fear and the anger swam through her, even to her hair.

There was a lot of talk. Everybody seemed determined to fill the room with it. Edwin said that his woman friend was also his office assistant. She had yellow hair arranged so that it hung from the crown of her head in fat curls. She wanted to know where Kitty's home was.

Kitty pointed to a window. "Out there. But it won't do you any good to look. You can't see it from here."

Yellow Hair asked what grade Kitty was in.

"I was supposed to have graduated from the second grade when the rest of them did," said Kitty. "But I didn't. I've got to go back and do it again."

"I'm sure you'll make it next time," sympathized Yellow Hair.

Edwin's man friend said that it didn't hurt nobody to fail once in a while, that before he got to where he was at he must have failed at least half a dozen times, but just look at where he was at now. Everybody laughed.

Kitty laughed when she thought she was supposed to laugh. Grinning, she sat in a corner staring at all of the excitement. She sucked her lower lip, rolled her eyes, and every few seconds or so pressed her stomach with her hands. It was making hungry noises. She hoped that Edwin's friends would think that she wasn't bright so they wouldn't ask any more questions.

Edwin didn't have anything else to say to her. He had brought Bauma an orchid in a little transparent box. Bauma said it was the first time anyone had given her anything so exotic. She and Edwin went into the bedroom for a short talk. They kept their voices low.

Kitty sat in her corner, and presently Edwin and his friends brought four pieces of luggage out of the bedroom and carried them from the house to the waiting car. Kitty's mother emerged from the bedroom. The orchid was pinned to the shoulder of her dress. She took her gloves, a key, and a five-dollar bill from her handbag and handed the key and the bill to Kitty. "The five dollars is for you. The key is to the front door. Be sure to lock it when you go. Give the key to Aunt Petal. I have an extra one. Eat a good supper and get down to Aunt Petal's before dark. Mind Aunt Petal. Don't give her any trouble."

"You didn't say how long you would be gone," said Kitty. "And you didn't say if I'm going to live with you when you get back, or where I'm going to live."

Her mother's smile came, and went, and came again. She bent to lay her cheek against Kitty's. "We'll be gone about a week, and I'll decide about you when I get back. I don't think you'll be able to live here with Edwin and me because this house wasn't built for a family. But we'll talk about that when I get back. Then we'll do things together. Right now let me go. Let me be as happy as I've been unhappy. You want me to be happy, don't you?"

"I want everybody to be happy," said Kitty, although she didn't quite know what happy meant. Whenever she thought about happy in connection with herself she could never get to the part that said what it was. Others seemed to have a prescription for it, but she had never been given one, so during her time with the Fords she had written her own. Happy was when others were happy. Sometimes the prescription worked. It didn't now.

Her mother's perfume was making her eyes water. The minute she had the house to herself she went into the bathroom and scrubbed her face until it was red. She looked for some plain soap and a white towel, but everything was scented and either pink or lavender.

In the kitchen she looked in the refrigerator to see a dish of pickled beets, a grapefruit, a loaf of health bread, a carton of eggs and another of cottage cheese. She sprinkled sugar on the cottage cheese and, wandering from room to room, ate it from the box. In the bedroom she saw that the sheets on the unmade bed were pink satin. On the dresser was a jewelry chest overflowing with drugstore jewelry.

Unbeautiful room, so silent, so conceited, so filled with self, self, and self.

Listening to the silence, Kitty stood at the dresser collecting her thoughts. Fierce and in neat anger, they gathered and grew. Like Hubert's angel, they perched on her shoulder and whispered things in her ear.

Thought number one said, "Can you imagine? Edwin doesn't know about the annulment. Nothing has made him think about it. Nothing has made him think to go look and see if it's written down somewhere. But what if something did? And he found out? What would he do then?"

Thought number two answered, saying, "Then poof! No more Edwin. He would run. He'd kick Ma out. He wouldn't even let her work in his factory again. It would be finished. Ma would have to go sleep under a bridge."

The house was filling with that brown, vague look that comes between daylight and dark. Kitty left it and walked down Moon Lake Road to Aunt Petal's.

Cupped in its meadow, the lake in the distance looked different than it had looked in full daylight.

Chapter three

Aunt Petal's spare room was a sleeping porch with windows all around that could be raised or lowered, depending on whim or the weather. To reach it, it was necessary to pass first through a parlor, then a kitchen, and then a passageway.

The parlor was a stuffy, moody little cell with a bead curtain hanging in its doorway and small, high windows that looked out into nothing. The beads were all colors.

Aunt Petal said that the parlor was her wedding chapel, but then she put a finger in her mouth and laughed. "But it really doesn't do much for the soul, does it?"

Wanting her bed and wondering how much longer it would be before she could climb into it, Kitty said, "I don't know. Maybe tomorrow when I look at it again it will do something for mine." She had never thought about her soul. She didn't even know if she had one.

Aunt Petal was built like a thermometer, but even her slight weight made the boards in the parlor floor creak.

Her kitchen was something time had left behind. It had a nook containing a table and two short benches. There was an oaken icebox, cupboards that reached to the ceiling, and a cast-iron range.

Aunt Petal said that the range and the icebox were close to being antiques, if they weren't already. "But I wouldn't part with them. They help me live. Even in the hottest weather it takes only twenty-five pounds of ice a day for the icebox, and the fuel for the stove comes from the woods. The electric company has never had to tell Tom and me to either pay our bill or have our service shut off."

Kitty looked around for Tom but didn't see him.

"Tom is my great-nephew," said Aunt Petal. "I don't know where he is just now. He takes disappearing pills every evening about this time. He

40

lives with me because he's got five sisters and they devil him from morning till night. When he was a baby his oldest sister tried to give him away. He's twelve now. You see that table and those benches? Tom made them."

"I thought you got them at a furniture store," said Kitty. She didn't think any such thing. The table looked ready to lurch off, and the benches had woodpecker holes in them.

Aunt Petal herded Kitty from the kitchen into the passageway, along which doors stood open to reveal beds spread over with crazy quilts. Standing beside one bed there was a treadle sewing machine. Pushed to one side of the passageway was a table. Next to it and under it were stacks of cardboard boxes.

Aunt Petal explained the boxes. "There was a hobby store in town that was going out of business and the owner was supposed to leave the building as clean as he had found it. So he hired Tom and me to do the job. Only when we got through with it he couldn't pay us but a fraction of what he owed us, so we settled by taking what's in these boxes. There's clay and paint and I don't know what all here. There are some how-to books and some tools."

On the table was a collection of claywork animals: an elephant, a rooster, a turtle, a pig. Grubby, childish little pieces, all had dried and cracked. They looked as if they had been modeled by the Somehow method. Somehow my comb will stay up there on top of my head if it doesn't fall off, said the rooster's sunken eyes. The elephant had lost its tail and one of its ears.

In the open windows wind chimes tinkled, and through them crept the coolness of evening.

Night came, and in her bed on the open-air porch Kitty lay counting the notes of some feathered night singer, sorrowful and close and then far away. She thought of her father who was, or who was not, her father. She could recall the shape of him, his clothes, and the way he walked—but she couldn't remember the sound of his voice.

The night singer fell silent. The moon rose and looked in. The coolness of the night deepened, and Kitty wished for something warmer than her muslin sheet. Her bed had not been given a quilt. She slept.

During the night Aunt Petal came gliding in to close the windows and to spread and tuck in a light cotton blanket. She was a minute or two at this. When it was done she clicked the button on her flashlight and in the darkness bent to smooth Kitty's hair. "Are you asleep?"

Half into sleep and half out of it, Kitty stirred. "Not now."

"I want to tell you," murmured Aunt Petal, "that I was a lot like you when I was your age. I didn't have much of a family either, except a brother and a couple of cousins. I was sent to live with one of the cousins on her farm, but she didn't study me much. She said she studied life, but if she did I never caught her at it. We had one of those old mule-driven sorghum mills. My cousin was like the mule. The mule pulled the lever round and round but never got anywhere nearer the juice."

"I was cold," said Kitty. "The blanket feels good."

"But I lived," said Aunt Petal. "I grew up. So will you. Just don't cry about what others do to you."

"I never cry," said Kitty. "Never."

"It will be good for Tom and me to have somebody like you around. We've lived here for so long that we've almost forgotten about others. We need somebody like you," said Aunt Petal, and went away.

That was all and yet it wasn't. Something important had happened. Alone again, Kitty reached up to touch the place where Aunt Petal's hand had been. A tear came, and then another. Her heart was glowing.

At breakfast the next morning she gave Aunt Petal the clay head she had made. Huddled over his plate of fried eggs, Tom watched. Aunt Petal had to prompt him to say wasn't he glad to meet Kitty. His eyes matched his brown knitted cap. He said that he and Aunt Petal were going to the woods to pick blackberries and if Kitty wanted to go he'd find her a bucket.

Aunt Petal wasn't sure that she could accept Kitty's gift. "It's beautiful," she said. "And yes, of course I like it. Who wouldn't? But this is something you should keep for yourself."

Kitty set the head beside Aunt Petal's plate. "I can make another one for myself. I want you to have this one."

"It's lovely," said Aunt Petal. "I'll find a place for it in my chapel. No, on second thought I won't. I'll just leave it here for a while. My chapel is too dark and musty. Prayerfully," she said, "I'll have a real chapel someday. One with lots of light and fresh air."

"You could have one with lots of light and fresh air now if you'd do like I told you," said Tom. "We could cut them little windows out and put in big ones. Then you'd have all the light and air in there you want."

"We don't know how to cut out little windows and put in big ones," said Aunt Petal. "And aside from that, big windows cost too much."

"You should put them on our need list," said Tom. "So the next time we get a cleaning job to do we won't put anything ahead of them."

"I will put big windows on our need list," said Aunt Petal.

On the way through the woods to the berry patches she whistled, and stopped whistling to stoop and tenderly poke a flower winking in the early sunlight. The windflowers and violets had gone with the spring, but the summer flowers were everywhere and there were long trails of ground vine. "I wish my house was out here," said Aunt Petal.

The land tilted and then stretched out flat. The wind sang through the tops of pines and oaks. In an oak clearing there were stands of blackberry bushes loaded with wild, dark fruit. Aunt Petal hung her bucket on her arm and began plopping berries into it.

To do his picking Tom moved around to the far edge of the bramble. He was first to fill his bucket and came bouncing back to announce that he was finished and was going home.

"So soon?" said Aunt Petal. She didn't look up to see that he had lost his cap. Kitty did, and as she plucked, and swatted insects, and sweated, she looked for the cap but didn't find it. The morning was only half finished and her bucket only three-quarters full when Aunt Petal sent her home to put baking soda on her insect bites.

She found the soda in Aunt Petal's kitchen. Tom's bucket of berries sat on the table beside the clay head. The contents of the bucket claimed Kitty's attention for a second.

She found Tom in Aunt Petal's side yard. On his table under the oak tree he had spread a square of oilcloth, cloth side up. On it he had placed his claywork animals and was studying them. In a tragic voice he said, "They were for Aunt Petal. She wanted me to make them. But they're no good, so I'm going to take all of them to the lake and drown them."

Appraisingly, Kitty eyed the pig. "Pigs have snouts. Where is his?"

"He don't have one," said Tom. "He's a lemon, and I wish I had never thought of him."

"Lemons make lemonade," said Kitty. She didn't know what she meant by that, but thought that it sounded clever.

"Usually when I do something I do it right," asserted Tom. "You can ask Aunt Petal if I don't."

The moist baking soda on Kitty's insect bites had dried. With a fingernail she flicked off the little white pieces. "You lost your cap."

"I know it," said Tom. "When I get time I'll go look for it."

"I found it," said Kitty.

Tom jerked to life. "Where?" he cried.

"Where you put it. In the bottom of your berry bucket. Under the berries."

Tom yanked at the belt to his pants. They struck his legs at mid-calf. "I got to tell you about Aunt Petal and her berries," he said. "It isn't like she needs any more. We got jars and jars of them all made into jam. A whole closetful left over from last summer and the summer before that. I keep telling her we don't need any more, but she goes right on picking. Some days she stays out there all day. She forgets to come home and eat and I have to go after her."

Out on Moon Lake Road a truck loaded with bricks passed. Kitty followed it with her eyes until it disappeared. "Have you," she asked Tom, "ever been to the brick factory?"

"One time we went," answered Tom. "Aunt Petal asked them for some bricks they were going to throw out. They don't sell the bad ones. They give them to whoever wants to go after them. But they wouldn't give any to Aunt Petal. Mr. Edwin Johnson is mad at her because she won't sell him her house or her woods. All he wants the house for is so he can burn it down. He calls it a chicken coop. And all he wants the woods for is so he can dig up the clay that's in them to make some more bricks. He'd ruin the woods."

"Edwin Johnson is kin to me," commented Kitty.

Tom looked away. "He's nasty. When he goes by here in his car he sticks his tongue out and hollers ugly things. Aunt Petal laughs at him. She thinks he's funny. I don't think he's funny. If Aunt Petal would let me I'd put some sharp nails in the road for him to run over. Then he'd have some flat tires, and while he was fixing them I'd run out and punch him in his liver."

From a branch in the overhanging tree a blue

feather floated down. Kitty looked at it. "What did Aunt Petal want the bricks for?"

"We were going to build a room out here," said Tom. "A little one but with lots of light and air. It was going to be Aunt Petal's chapel."

Kitty rose, went out to the road, looked in the direction of the brick factory, and came back. She sat on her grassy seat, and after a little time of quiet she reached to touch Tom on his shoulder. "If you want to make some new animals for Aunt Petal, I'll help you."

Tom turned his head and spoke only with his eyes. After a second had ticked by, a smile came into them. It set the stage for the busy friendship days that came rolling up out of the east each morning to wake the great live oak in Aunt Petal's yard. The tree stood seventy feet high and its arched branches spread one hundred and thirty-eight feet across. A small house could easily fit under it.

The morning sun set its fiery gaze on the two youthful lunatics beneath the tree. The kid with the magnificent brown eyes thought that he was about to become one of the world's great sculptors, and the one with the pale hair was certain she was one of those special somebodies who could make a difference in the lives of others.

The sun observed yet another who looked out a door or a window once in a while and smiled a tolerant smile. She had given the side yard to the lunatics to make anything in it they wished. She knew about the passions of childhood, here today and gone tomorrow. Let them come. Let them make their harmless messes and lay their impossible plans. Tomorrow the dreams in them would be gone.

Aunt Petal closed her door and went back to her sewing. She was making a shirt for Tom and, having had a look at Kitty's clothes supply, was thinking that one for Kitty wouldn't be such a bad idea either. There was enough in the remnant for two.

Aunt Petal took her button bag from its drawer and began pawing through its contents, searching for six green buttons and six blue ones.

Beneath the champion live oak Kitty and Tom shook out grand plans. More truly, Kitty shook out her grand plans. "I'm going to make a wild garden out here and if you'll make some animals we can set them around in it. Think of how it will look. Think of how glad it will make Aunt Petal."

Tom asked no questions. Glad to be rid of his mistakes, he took all of his old animals over to Moon Lake and tossed them in.

Left alone, Kitty went around to the back of the house and found a short-handled spade. In the side yard she chose a spot away from the tree for the wild plants that would be brought from the woods and planted in borders. From their clean leaves and colors Tom's animals would peer out, and seeing them, the couples who came to be married would smile. They would tell others and others would come.

Good ideas, those. They would make a difference. But there was yet another idea that was even better.

Kitty set the tip of her spade in a mound of loosened earth and lay in the grass with her arms over her face.

The brick factory had a whistle that blew at noon and again at four-thirty. The noon whistle was blowing then.

Chapter four

*T*he day after Tom sent his failed animals to their watery graves, he declared his intention to make a fresh start. Setting up shop under the oak, he lugged the benches from the kitchen and brought a plastic pail and set it on the worktable. The pail had an airtight lid and contained a good-sized lump of clay wrapped in plastic to keep it moist.

Gallantly Tom chose the bench with the most woodpecker holes in it for himself.

Today Kitty's creative juices were playing

hooky. So were the plans for the wild garden, still mostly in the think stage. None of the plants for it had yet been brought from the woods. Furrows of turned earth lay waiting for them, but there was no hurry. Other things had to come first.

On her bench, Kitty watched a car come down Moon Lake Road headed in the direction of the factory. Abreast of Aunt Petal's place, it slowed for an instant. Its driver looked out and didn't return Kitty's wave. He jerked back, the car gave a leap and sped on. Kitty put her tongue in her cheek.

Tom took no notice of the car. All steamed up, he couldn't wait to get at the clay. He wanted to make a lion, a turkey, a bull. He was in a fever to make a model of his own head.

Kitty took command. "Make the animals first. Then we'll make the head."

"I want it to look like me," said Tom. "Strong."

"When we make it, it will look like you," said Kitty. "Strong." She thought that Tom had an interesting mind. She didn't think that his face was especially strong, except when he was objecting to Aunt Petal doing things he thought unbefitting. Then his jaw hardened and his mouth thinned to a sharp line.

Aunt Petal had a grocery cart such as those used in food markets. Early every morning she wheeled it out, saying that she was perfectly capable of going after the daily block of ice for her icebox and why couldn't she?

Tom would not allow it. "That is not a lady's job," he said. And each day he took the cart away from her and went after the ice himself. He would not allow Aunt Petal to gather firewood or pound a nail if one needed to be pounded. A lady picked blackberries if that's what she wanted to do. She cooked and read books. A walk to town to pay a bill or buy some thread befitted a lady, but she must wear her hat, her white gloves, and her pearl brooch so that everybody would know she was one.

This morning, having been after the ice and having waved Aunt Petal off to town, Tom was ready to start becoming what he knew he could become. From the pail at his elbow he pulled the lump of clay, set it on the oilcloth, peeled away its plastic covering, and picked up his cutting wire. "Now don't talk to me," he said. "I am going to make a bull."

Kitty left him and walked up the road to her mother's house.

Still in her pajamas and robe, Bauma asked Kitty into her dining room. The remains of a skimpy breakfast for two and sheets of wadded notepaper littered its table.

"I saw Edwin go past Aunt Petal's, so I knew you were back," said Kitty.

"I was going to call you," said her mother. "But I wanted to try and write a letter to your father first. Did you tell me he was in Colorado?"

"That's what Brother told me," said Kitty.

"Whose brother?"

"His name was Brother."

"Nobody's name is Brother."

"His was. And his sister's name was Sister. I don't know what else. They didn't tell me. I saw them that day I went to my father's house. They came by."

"Did they tell you the name of the town where your father could be reached in case he was needed?"

"It was just Brother who did all the talking," said Kitty. "And all he said was my father went to Colorado to see mountains. Sister only said a few words. She kept screaming for Brother to come on, come on. She had on a pair of her mother's shoes. They were green. She had cute legs. Brother was wearing glasses. They had gold rims."

"All right, all right," said her mother. "I don't want to hear all of that. It's not doing me any good. Have you had your breakfast?"

"Sure," said Kitty. "Hours ago. Aunt Petal's gone to town to pay a bill and buy some thread. Yesterday she made blackberry jam. It's better than what you can buy in a store." There was some spilled sugar on the table and Kitty nudged it into a little pile and then onto a saucer. "Are we going to do things together today?"

"What?" said her mother. The diamonds on her left hand sparkled.

"You said when you got back from Texas we'd do things together," said Kitty.

"Oh, not today," said her mother. "Can't you see I'm up to my eyebrows in all I have to do today?"

"I thought you were just sitting here writing a letter," said Kitty.

"I *am* just sitting here writing a letter," said her mother. The sheet of paper in front of her was blank. She pulled it toward her and set the tip of her pen down on it hard but didn't write anything. "If there's anything I hate it's having to write to your father. It shouldn't be necessary. You're as much his responsibility as you are mine."

"Aunt Petal is making me a new shirt," said Kitty.

"You'd think he would have had the common decency to let me know where I could reach him," said her mother. "But no, not that one. He never heard of common decency. I suppose the only thing for me to do is write to him at his address in Cottonville and hope the letter will be forwarded."

"Denver is in Colorado," reflected Kitty.

"That's the capital and it's got mountains. So why don't you send your letter to Denver?"

Her mother looked at her. "Brilliant. Why didn't I think of that? There must be only about several million people in Denver, so I'm sure the post office there wouldn't have any trouble locating your father, he's so important."

"But I don't know," Kitty went on. "Colorado is full of mountains. Maybe my father isn't in Denver."

Her mother wrote the date on the sheet of notepaper and laid her pen down. She wouldn't be caught dead without that stuff on her eyelids to make her eyes look more purple than they are, thought Kitty. To get her own way with my father she knew how to bat those eyes and how to throw a first-class fit when he wouldn't let her have it. She did it to Hubert too. Oh, the lies she used to tell that poor old sock. Nobody snatched her purse that day with all the grocery money in it. She lost it playing cards with her friends. And then there were those times she would lock me in a room, run off, and be gone all day. She'd beat Hubert home by about twenty minutes, scrub all her makeup off, drag her dair down, and tell him the reason nothing was done was because her heart was hurting her again. Then he'd take all of us out to eat hot dogs. Boy, the shockers she used to tell Hubert, and now she lies about him. She's no slouch when it comes to lying about me either, but right now I'm her hot potato and what is she going to do about me?

Kitty craned her neck to look past her mother through a door that led to a small room jutting off from the hallway. "I didn't notice till just now that this house has got two bedrooms."

"It hasn't," said her mother quickly.

"I see two," said Kitty.

"That little room is not a bedroom," said her mother. "It's Edwin's den."

She's so pretty, thought Kitty. I wish I could love her. I wish I could like her. I wish I was Wilhelmenia Von Zock or even Mildred Sack. "If I could come and live with you, you could put a little bed in there for me. When Edwin wanted it to be his den I could go someplace else. I could go to a movie or someplace like that."

Her mother picked up her pen and wrote two words on her sheet of notepaper. "Edwin doesn't like children. You would create too much of a disturbance, and I couldn't have it. Aren't you comfortable at Aunt Petal's?"

"Not very," said Kitty. She was supremely comfortable at Aunt Petal's. "I am not very comfortable at Aunt Petal's," she said.

Her mother tried to hide her annoyance with this new trouble. "What is making you uncomfortable?"

"There's nothing to do," said Kitty. "Except go to the woods and pick blackberries. Every day, because there's nothing much else to do, Tom and I go to the woods with Aunt Petal and pick blackberries. Tom is her great-nephew."

"I know who he is," said her mother.

"He's got a lot of sisters and they devil him from morning till night. One time his father was digging a cellar and it filled up with water. Tom fell in it and almost was drowned. He was just a little baby then. His oldest sister jumped in and saved him. Then she tried to give him away. She had on her best dress that day and she's been mad at him ever since. That's why he lives with Aunt Petal. Also because Aunt Petal might have a fire at her house someday, and if he didn't live with her he wouldn't be there to put it out," said Kitty.

Her mother had written four lines and was dissatisfied with them. She held her pen against her cheek and drew back into the protective softness of her robe. "Must you drag your stories out so? I asked you what was making you uncomfortable at Aunt Petal's."

"It's the blackberries and the woods," lamented Kitty. "Every day it's so hot out there in the woods it's like frying. Everything sticks and bites. Then we go home and make jam. I like to do things, but not picking blackberries and making jam. When I lived with the Fords we didn't do stuff like that. We did interesting things. For instance we had parties."

Her mother made no response to that. She slid forward in her chair and wrote two more lines.

After a moment Kitty whacked the table with her fist and cried, "Ma! I know! Let's you and Edwin and me have a party. You can get all your friends to come and I'll help. I'll put the little sandwiches on the trays and pass them around. If anybody spills anything I'll run get the mop and clean it up. I'll make the ice cubes for the iced tea and put cherries and pieces of lemon in them."

This time her mother had a quick response. "No. I can't think about parties now. Listen here. I've just remarried and I've got a thousand things on my mind. I'm just home from a long trip and haven't even unpacked yet. I've got that to do and I've got this letter to write. Listen here. When I was your age I wasn't always hounding my mother to do things with me. I did things by myself. I invented things to keep myself busy. Can't you do that?"

Kitty hooked her heels over the rung of her chair. "Sure. I can do that. I know how to invent things to do. I've already got one thing invented. In my mind. It's big and would keep me busy a long time. I've got some trouble with it though."

"What trouble?" asked her mother. The expression on her face said that she was ready to satisfy any trouble if only the one in front of her would fly away.

"It'll take some bricks," said Kitty.

Relief flooded her mother's face. "That's no trouble. Edwin gives his imperfect bricks away to anybody who wants to go after them. Aunt Petal has a cart. I've seen her pushing it up and down the road. Borrow it and you and Tom go after all the bricks you want. I'll call Edwin and tell him you're coming."

"I don't mean pieces of ones that have cracks in them," said Kitty. "My invention is going to be a special project. Very special. So I need nice whole bricks, perfect ones."

"I will tell Edwin that you need some perfect bricks," said her mother. "Do you want to go after them now, or when? Tell me and let's get through with this."

Kitty set her feet on the floor. "Could Edwin bring them to me? I need a whole bunch. I couldn't haul all I need in Aunt Petal's cart. They'd be too heavy."

Her mother rose and went to the kitchen to use the telephone. It hung on the wall on the other side of the refrigerator, so the conversation with Edwin was muffled.

Edwin came with a load of bricks that afternoon. It was close to five o'clock and Moon Lake Road was empty of the four-thirty homegoing factory traffic. Back from town and putting supper off for an hour, Aunt Petal napped in her bedroom.

At their table under the oak tree Kitty and

Tom were discussing the merits and demerits of Tom's bull. Tom was defending it, but broke off in the middle of his argument to say, "There comes Mr. Edwin Johnson."

Kitty heard the truck turn in but didn't look up. "What I was saying was, you're going too fast. This bull isn't going to look like a bull. It's going to look like one of those long dogs. What are these lumps stuck on here? Legs? Bulls don't have such short legs. These legs are too fat and they're too close together. If these front ones could talk they would say to each other, 'You let me by this time and I'll let you by the next.' "

Tom was not listening to her. His attention was riveted on the oncoming truck. "Yes sir, that's Mr. Edwin Johnson. Look at him jerk that truck. He's mad. He's going to tear his truck up, he's so mad. He's after our house and the woods again. He's making ruts in our grass. This time I'm going to tell him. We don't want to sell him our house or the woods and he can get off our property. It's private."

The truck continued to move toward the tree. When it reached the point where it would have to take its chances with the low, outflung branches it bumped to a stop. Edwin got out.

Tom was on his feet, shaking his fist at Edwin and screaming. "If you're after Aunt Petal's house and the woods again, you can get on down the road where you belong! She don't want you to dig up the woods and ruin them just so you can have some more clay pits, and she's going to live in her house till she dies, so you can just go on and leave us alone!"

Edwin wasted only a glance on Tom. He looked at Kitty as if he wanted to bite her, as if she might be something bitter in his mouth and he couldn't find any place to spit it out. "Bauma said you wanted some bricks."

"They're for a project I've got in mind," said Kitty.

"I've brought you some," said Edwin.

"We don't want none of your bricks!" shouted Tom. "We don't want nothing from you!"

There weren't nearly enough bricks on the back of Edwin's truck for Kitty's project, but she said, "I want them. Aunt Petal said I could make anything I wanted to out here, and I need the bricks."

Edwin didn't ask where she wanted them. He went around to the back of the truck and began the unloading job.

Balefully Tom watched and cheerfully Kitty looked on. "I went to see Bauma today," she told Edwin. "I thought I could go live with you and her, but she said your house is too small for three people."

"Yes, it's too small for three people," said Edwin. "It's only got one bedroom."

"It's got a den," said Kitty.

"That's where I do the work that I have to take home from the office," said Edwin. He didn't look up from his brick stacking.

Tom had gone to the house. He returned from it carrying a damp towel. Right or wrong, he covered his day's work with the towel and said he had to go build the supper fire and wake Aunt Petal. He took up his bench and stalked back to the house, turning when he reached its door to send a last warning scowl in Edwin's direction.

Edwin finished stacking the bricks, peeled off his work gloves, and slapped them against his thigh. "There. That ought to fix you up with your project."

"I hope it will keep me busy," said Kitty. "If it does I won't have time to hound Bauma to do things with me. I make her nervous, but she is an angel, isn't she?"

"She certainly is," agreed Edwin.

"I know a man who carries an angel around with him," commented Kitty. "It talks to him."

"Is that so?" said Edwin.

"Sometime I'll tell you about him," promised Kitty.

"You do that," said Edwin. He had been careful about setting the bricks under the tree. He wasn't so careful when he drove off. He took the turn onto Moon Lake Road too quickly and for several minutes was stuck in the soft sand of its shoulder.

Watching him maneuver, watching the truck wheels spin, Kitty sat on her bench clasping her hands. Never empty of the past and now throbbing with the present too, her heart wanted to laugh or cry, it didn't know which. But then in her head the facts of the past and the present sounded a cracking blow and her short laugh came.

At supper Aunt Petal asked what the bricks in the yard were for. "Mr. Edwin Johnson brought them to Kitty," said Tom. "They're for a project she's got in mind, but she won't say what it is."

"When I was a child I played with dominoes," remarked Aunt Petal. "But I guess times have changed. Now it's bricks."

Tom dropped his soup spoon and had to leave the table to get a clean one. When he came back to the table he slurped the rest of his soup very fast.

Aunt Petal said that his manners belonged in a stable and that if they didn't improve he could henceforth take his meals in his room. Her own soup went untouched. Nibbling at a slice of bread, she said that the cost of things in town was enough to make your ma hit your pa. "Nowadays a person like me has two kinds of chances," she said. "Slim and none." Hopefully, she listened to the sound of each passing car. Hopefully, she watched the clock saying that it was the marrying hour, but nobody came.

So presently Aunt Petal gave up watching and

listening. She said that her day in town had about done her up, but before she went to her early bed she telephoned Kitty's mother. It was decided that Kitty would stay on with her. "At least for the rest of the summer," Aunt Petal said. She was pleased. Her pleasure was genuine. It showed in her eyes. But she was sick.

Chapter five

Her sickness was the short-term summer flu, but Aunt Petal did not call it that. She said it was the ague. She slept long hours, and woke, and slept again. The sight of food only made her sicker, she said.

Tom lost interest in his claywork. Muttering to himself, he crept through the house, pausing in the parlor long enough to observe its dreariness with bitter eyes. He lived for Aunt Petal's call and would not leave the house except to go for ice, fresh foods, and firewood. At mealtimes he built the fire in the stove.

What came from the stove at mealtimes discouraged even Tom's healthy appetite. Kitty's poor man's gravy—browned ground meat in what was supposed to be a cream gravy—was so thick it had to be plopped from the pan. Unmoving, it lay on the boiled potatoes and bread slices as if it might be protecting them from something.

Tom pushed his plate away, left the table, and returned with a bowl of fresh blackberries. "They're all going to sour if we don't eat them," he said.

The birds in the side yard discovered Tom's towel spread over his claywork. With their beaks they plucked and pulled at it. One, with a string in its mouth, flew off to the stack of bricks.

It was morning, the third day Aunt Petal had kept to her room. Looking out at the bricks, Kitty said to Tom, "I wish somebody would come."

Frying bacon, Tom said, "Nobody's going to come. Since Mr. Edwin Johnson had the county take the bumps out of the road people don't have to slow down when they go past here. They don't stop anymore to buy our jam or berries. They don't come to get married anymore either. Aunt Petal is better at marrying than a preacher, but they want it to look like a church with flowers and all and it don't."

"I think a doctor should come," said Kitty.

Tom bristled. "Another time when Aunt Petal had the ague we got a doctor to come, and he said she shouldn't live here with only me to take care of her. So this time she don't want no doctor. She only wants me, and I know what to do. I can take care of her. The oven's hot now. Are you going to make them drop biscuits to go with this bacon?"

Kitty made the biscuits, and she and Tom took two buttered ones and three slices of the bacon in to Aunt Petal. Ruefully she looked at her plate. "I can't eat."

"You've got to," urged Tom. "You'll die if you don't."

Aunt Petal raised up long enough to flop her pillow over. "If you're trying to scare me, you are wasting your time. People die every day and so far as I know, they don't have any bad aftereffects. What day is it?"

"It's Friday," answered Kitty. Aunt Petal's white face made her want to howl. She thought of the two times in her life she herself had been sick. Both had been during her stay with the Fords. To help make her well she had been reminded of all the good things waiting for her. Thinking about them had worked better than all the pills she had been made to swallow. But what if there hadn't been any? If there had been only jam and blackberries that nobody wanted to buy, if there had been only the waiting and watching for somebody to come, if the promises of good things hadn't been real, would she have been so glad for another day?

Concealing her wrath over the realities of Aunt Petal's shaky world, Kitty straightened the sheet covering Aunt Petal's feet. "I am making a wild garden in your yard. When it's finished you won't have to go to the woods to see the flowers and pretty plants."

"One of you take the plate away, and both of you go away and let me alone," said Aunt Petal. She found some energy. "If it's Friday, it's washday. Tom, can you manage the washing?"

"Nothing's dirty," said Tom.

"Those pants you have on certainly are," said Aunt Petal. "If you fell down in them, you wouldn't stop sliding."

"They're just right," protested Tom. "Before I decided to wear them again today, I gave them my test. I threw them up against the wall and they didn't stick."

Aunt Petal closed her eyes. "Go wash them. Take all the sheets off the beds and all the used towels from the bathroom and wash them. Wash everything."

So for Tom it was washday on Aunt Petal's back porch; a large, vigorous proceeding. In the relic machine the towels and sheets churned in soapy water. Groaning and shaking, as if intoxicated, the machine balked at so much work. It washed but would not rinse. Tom loaded what had been washed into a basket, lugged it out to the clothesline, hung the pieces, and hosed them down. He said that it was his job, that he would do it and didn't want Kitty's help.

Kitty rolled Aunt Petal's cart out and went to the woods to dig clumps of Boston fern and white-rayed asters. In what was to become Aunt Petal's wild garden she set them in the furrows she had prepared. She patted the earth around their roots, watered them, and left them to their growing.

With what was left of the wash water, Tom was scrubbing the back porch. Side by side his pants and Aunt Petal's nightshirts blew on the clothesline. In her sleep Aunt Petal lay on her side with her face turned to the wall.

Kitty pushed her hair up off her hot neck and went to the Johnson house to see her mother about the bumps in Moon Lake Road. Or, more accurately, the bumps that were not in Moon Lake Road.

Her mother now had a maid, a young, fresh-cheeked slip of a girl, the kind seen in country yards on Sunday afternoons. Importantly she answered the doorbell, and with an anxious smile said that she was Shelley Ruth, Mrs. Johnson's maid, that Mrs. Johnson wasn't up yet, and what did Kitty want?

"I'm Mrs. Johnson's cousin and I want to see her about some road bumps I need," said Kitty.

Shelley Ruth didn't see anything unusual in that. She said she didn't know if Mrs. Johnson was receiving, but if Kitty wanted to come in, she would go and find out.

There was new furniture in the living room: a leather sofa and chairs to match, a wide-screened television set, a glass-topped table. On the table there was a crystal fish. The bowl of artificial fruit was gone. The photograph of Kitty's mother still looked down from a wall. It had a new frame.

The door to the bedroom was closed. Shelley Ruth went to it, knocked on it, went in, and came back out. "Mrs. Johnson will receive you now," she announced.

Curiously Kitty studied the innocence of Shelley Ruth, and asked a tender question. "How old are you?"

"Nineteen," breathed Shelley Ruth. "And I've never worked out before. Before, my work was helping Mama with the little kids. This is my first paying job. Mama got it for me. I hope I'm doing it right."

"You're doing it right," said Kitty, and went in to see her mother who was propped up in her bed on satin pillows. She looked rested and healthy, but at once began to tell Kitty that she was neither. "I didn't sleep well last night. That's the reason I came back to bed after I got Edwin off to work. Getting him off to work in the mornings utterly exhausts me. I'm beginning to wonder if I might be anemic, I feel so exhausted in the mornings."

Kitty made herself comfortable on the foot of her mother's bed. Having heard lectures at school about one way people become anemic, she said, "Hookworms."

"What?" said her mother.

"There was a girl at school who was anemic," said Kitty. "Caused by hookworms. She went barefooted a lot around where an outside toilet and some dogs had been. There were some hookworms in the ground, and they crawled up on her feet and made holes in them. Then they crawled up into her intestines and sucked her blood. So she was anemic."

"I never go barefooted," said her mother, horrified. "Especially I don't where there are outside toilets or where dogs have been. I don't like dogs."

"Then maybe you aren't anemic," consoled Kitty. "Maybe you've got the ague. Aunt Petal's got it."

"The what?" said her mother.

"The ague. It's like a bad cold or flu. You get weak and don't eat. Aunt Petal has been sick for three days now."

"I have not got the ague," said her mother. "I am just tired, but I can't rest because everybody wants something from me. Edwin wants me to get up and eat breakfast with him every morning, so I have to do that. He talks and talks. About bricks and his mother's cooking. When we were in Texas she spent all of her time cooking for him. We didn't go out to a restaurant once. He wanted what his mother cooked. Nothing fried. Stuff that takes hours to put together and has to be watched. You'd think knowing how to cook like his mother cooks was some kind of a virtue the way he talks about it. Since we got back that's all he talks about in the mornings. That and bricks. I have told him a dozen times I don't like to talk in the mornings, but he can't understand that. He's like his mother. She talks and sings. When we were in Texas I couldn't get away from her talking and singing. Her singing was the worst I ever heard. Awful. If there's anything I can't stand, it's somebody who thinks she can sing when she can't."

"At Aunt Petal's we talk while we're eating breakfast, but nobody sings," said Kitty.

Her mother jerked one of the pillows out from under her head and threw it onto the floor. "And that idiot Shelley Ruth keeps running in here with questions a moron would be ashamed to ask. The only time I get any rest from her is when she leaves at three o'clock. She doesn't know how to answer the phone. I have to get up and do it."

"Why don't you have another one put in

here?" asked Kitty. "I remember we had two phones when you were married to Hubert. The one he had put beside your bed looked like gold. It wasn't, but it looked like it was. Hubert is a sweet old sock."

In the living room Shelley Ruth was running a vacuum cleaner. Its whine went past the closed bedroom door and moved away. In the wake of it Kitty's mother said, "Edwin won't let me have a phone put in here. He calls his mother every night and she wants the conversations private."

"One in here wouldn't have to be hooked up to the one in the kitchen," reasoned Kitty. "It could be extra. Probably if Edwin knew Hubert gave you an extra phone he'd get you one in a minute, he'd be so jealous."

There was a short silence. Then her mother said, "I ought to get up, but honestly I don't have the energy."

Kitty lifted the pillow from the floor, placed it on her lap, set her elbows in it, and put her face in her hands. "Maybe," she suggested, "you're pregnant."

As if a hunk of ceiling had fallen on her, her mother got out of bed fast, went to the dresser, seized a brush, and with swift strokes began brushing her hair. "I am not pregnant. I am not going to be pregnant. I don't want another child."

You didn't want me, but here I am, thought

Kitty. "Your hair is so pretty," she said. "I wish mine was like yours."

Her mother continued her brushing. "Your hair was always the despair of my life," she said. "Nice hair needs attention, the same as anything else nice if you want to keep it that way, but I was never able to din that into you. You're like your father. No pride in your personal appearance. Well, I take pride in mine. It pays."

Kitty dropped her hands and put the pillow aside. Conversations with her mother never failed to make her feel that she was an ugly accident that had slipped past the notice of whoever was in charge of preventing ugly accidents. "The reason I'm here," she said. "is we need the bumps put back in the road. Will you ask Edwin to do it?"

In the middle of a stroke, her mother's hand stopped its motion. As though it had been grabbed by another unseen one, it hung suspended about four inches above her head. The lace falling over its wrist was frothy white. "Did I hear you say you want me to ask Edwin to put the bumps back in the road? What bumps? What road?"

"The bumps in Moon Lake Road," said Kitty. "Edwin had the county take them out, but we need them put back so when people go past Aunt Petal's they'll have to slow down. So they'll see the sign that says Aunt Petal performs marriages and the one that says about the blackberries for sale. Then they'll stop and get married or buy something. Like the road is now, there's nothing to slow anybody down, so they don't see the signs and they go on."

Kitty's mother remembered her hand and the brush. She lowered both to the dresser top, and, as if she might draw something from it, leaned to look at the reflection of her face in the mirror above the dresser.

Kitty tasted her slow smile. "I thought of calling Edwin myself to ask him to do it, but then I thought if he didn't answer his phone, if his assistant did, she would want to know who I was and maybe I would have told her he was my new Pa. I might have done that. It might have slipped out."

The mirror hadn't given Kitty's mother what she was looking for. She gave up her search, turned, and set her back against the dresser.

"So I think it would be better if you did it," said Kitty. "Don't you?"

There was frosty stillness in the eyes that looked back at her. The mouth that went with them spoke. "I don't know what I think I'm too tired to think. I'm going back to bed. There's a check for Aunt Petal on the refrigerator door. Take it to her, and on your way out tell Shelley Ruth to bring me a glass of water and an aspirin, will you?"

This was not a request, it was a dismissal, unyielding, even hostile. Because it was a luxury her mother could not afford, the hostility would not last. Of that Kitty was confident. Her mother was president of the Society of Accomplished Liars, but she was no dummy.

Pleased with what she was certain her visit with her mother would bring, Kitty went back to Aunt Petal's. On the way she left the road to skip through meadows, stopping here and there to look at lichens growing on a rock, a field lizard, some field insects, some weed blades. Affectionately she patted the rock. Across the meadows and above Moon Lake Road heat waves danced. On the road there was no unusual activity. None was expected because today was already half gone.

Today Tom took his laundry in. He and Kitty spread the sun-warmed sheets on the beds and fluffed the pillows. Aunt Petal got out of her bed long enough to take a bath.

Following Aunt Petal's instructions, Kitty cooked white beans, flavoring them with onions and a slab of fatback. Aunt Petal said she thought some fresh fruit would go good with the beans, so Tom took money from one of her sewing machine drawers and tore off to the country store. He came back with a watermelon, and Aunt Petal ate a slice of it and a bowl of the beans.

When the last supper dish had been washed and put away and the fire in the stove had died, Kitty took a book of stories from a shelf in the parlor and went in to read to Aunt Petal. Tom sat on the floor beside Aunt Petal's bed, holding her hand and pretending to listen. He smiled when she smiled and grunted when she grunted.

The story Kitty read was old and wordy. In the beginning of it the hero was not a very likely lad. He didn't do much except look at the lambent moon afar and write poetry. But then he got going. Everything got going. Nobody was quiet. The hero blossomed. It was revealed that he had a red mustache that drooped down over his youthful mouth and that the muscles in his arms were like bands of steel. When he proclaimed his love for the heroine it made a noise like a plate-glass window crashing to the sidewalk. He told the heroine that as soon as they were wed they would go traveling.

The heroine's father heard that and came charging out to roar, "You're wrong, my boy! You'll go right now instead!"

So the hero went traveling by himself, out through the door, pieces two by four. So it wasn't a happy ending. Aunt Petal said it made her feel cozy. "That girl wasn't right for him anyway. She was too much of a daddy's pet. I would have told him so if he had come and asked me."

Kitty closed the book. Tom rose and pulled

Aunt Petal's sheet up around her neck. He kissed her and felt her forehead. He said it wasn't too hot or too cold and maybe the ague was gone. Aunt Petal said it wasn't, that she would know when it was. She threw the sheet back and pushed Tom away.

Before she turned off the light on the sleeping porch that night, Kitty wrote a letter to Cook saying where she was, and that nothing bad was happening to her. She told Cook about Aunt Petal and her ague, saying she thought the ague was over, but that Aunt Petal didn't want it to be.

Chapter six

*T*omorrow came. In the early morning of it Aunt Petal ate what Tom and Kitty took to her, but she didn't want her newspaper and wouldn't get out of bed. She and Tom had words.

"If it was me who had been sick, you'd make me get up," said Tom. "The longer somebody who has been sick stays in bed, the weaker he gets. That's what you say to me after I've been sick."

"You've never had the ague," said Aunt Petal.

"You haven't got it now," fumed Tom. "It's gone. So why don't you get up and move around some? Why don't you come out into the yard with Kitty and me? I'm making clay animals and Kitty is making a wild garden. You don't have to put on your clothes. You can come out in your nightshirt."

"If I had the strength to get out of bed, don't you think I'd have enough left over to put on my clothes?" snapped Aunt Petal. "I may be old and simple, but I'm not so far gone that I'm going to walk around outside in my nightshirt."

"Who said you were old and simple?" demanded Tom.

"They don't have to say it," said Aunt Petal. "It's enough that they think it. I know what people think about me. Every time I go to town I'm reminded. I've had plenty of time these last few days to think about what people think about me, and they're right. I'm a daffy old lady who has got no business living out here by herself. I belong where the rest of the old folks live. In a home. Where somebody can tell me what time to get up and what time to go to bed and what to eat and what not to eat. So I've decided to go to one of those places. You'd better write to your father and tell him to come and get you."

"You'd better not tell me to do that," warned Tom. "I might do it and then where would you be?"

"Where I belong," said Aunt Petal. "In an old folks' home. I've made up my mind to quit on this one. If Edwin Johnson still wants to buy it and my woods, tell him he can have them. You can have the money. Use it for your education. Go to college and learn something. Maybe what you learn won't be too much for you to carry around."

"What if an old folks' home won't let you in unless you pay them to stay there?" said Tom. "If you give me all your money, you won't have any to pay them with."

"They can have my brooch," said Aunt Petal. "If they want more than it's worth, they can charge it to the dust and let the rain settle it."

Tom went to a window and with a hard swat of his palm made the wind chime hanging in it tinkle. He took his worry and anger to the yard where he lifted the towel covering his claywork and eyed what was underneath. He had forgotten to keep the towel damp. The birds had pecked holes in it and made off with chunks of his dehydrated bull.

Breaking ground for the showy pine lilies yet to come from the woods, Kitty said, "You should have kept the towel damp and should have covered the whole thing up with a box to keep the birds away."

Tom swept what was left of his bull into a heap. His mouth was grim. "And you should do whatever you're going to do with those bricks. Why don't you put them around the flowerbeds? That's what you got them for, isn't it? So why don't you do it? They're not going to jump up and do it themselves."

Kitty came to stand her shovel against the trunk of the tree. She sat in the grass examining her dirty hands and knees. The soil in the woods was red-flecked where bits of clay had washed up to the black topsoil from subterranean storehouses.

It was confidence time. "The bricks," Kitty told Tom, "are not to put around the flowerbeds. As soon as I get enough of them I'm going to build a playhouse. Out here. Under this tree. One room. With a nice roof and big windows so it will have lots of light and air."

In the flowerbeds, those that had been established, the asters peeped out to drink the wide air and nod to their bedfellows, the ferns.

"And when I don't live here anymore," announced Kitty, "the playhouse I'm going to build can be Aunt Petal's chapel."

Tom had the ability to accept the sudden. He took his breath in and let it out. "Does Mr. Edwin Johnson know you're going to need some more bricks?"

"Not yet," said Kitty.

"When are you going to tell him?"

"Soon."

"Are you going to tell him what you're going to do with them?"

"Sure."

"Do you know how to build a playhouse?"

"No."

"Then how are you going to build one?"

"I'm not going to build it. Somebody else is going to do that."

"Who?"

"I don't know. Somebody. A man. My cousins will send somebody."

Tom's face was shining. He sprang from his bench. "I'm going to tell Aunt Petal. Let me be the one to tell her."

"She's asleep," said Kitty. "I just looked. Sit down. You've got work to do. Anyway it's too early to tell her. We should wait till the rest of the bricks come."

"You are weird," said Tom, but he said it as a compliment, and Kitty began to tell him about another idea she had. She had been thinking and thinking about how she was going to tell Edwin about Hubert. Now she thought she knew how she was going to do it. She began to tell Tom about the clay angel she was going to make. "I know a man who has an angel. It rides around on his shoulder. It's not real, but he thinks it is. It talks to him. It's beautiful. Mine will be beautiful."

"It will go with the animals," declared Tom. "So cute. All of them sitting there where the plants are."

"My angel is not to go with the animals," said Kitty. "It's to give to Edwin to thank him for what he does for us. I'll tell him where I got the idea. From that man I know."

Out on Moon Lake Road two flatbed trucks were passing. Kitty turned to watch them. Just above the lane leading into Aunt Petal's place they turned around and came back to stop at a spot below the "Blackberries for Sale" sign and the one that advertised "Marriages Performed."

Tom watched for only a second. Turning his back on the whole thing, he lifted a ball of clay from its pail. To remove any air bubbles that might be in it, he threw it down hard onto the table, lifted it again, and threw it down again. Then he took up his cutting wire, sliced into the clay, separating it so that there were two parts, and began to slap the parts together. He was going to make an animal, but not a bull this time. Bulls didn't have style. Neither did pigs, What had style?

"Horses have style," said Kitty, still watching the trucks.

By this time five men had climbed out of them. They wore orange hats and orange vests. They looked at the flawless sky, shook their disappointed heads, and shuffled around to the backs of the trucks. One of them jumped up and handed down tools and orange roadworking signs, but not until a man in a white pickup arrived did any work begin. Then there was no more standing around leaning on shovels and swapping gab. The road was blocked off with the signs and the work on it began.

Kitty went back to her own shoveling. Tom left his work to go check on Aunt Petal and find a picture of a stylish horse. He said he didn't care what was being done to the road, but he couldn't stay away from it. After an hour of pretended indifference he ran down the lane to watch. He came galloping back with an excited report. "They're putting the bumps back!"

Kitty asked, "Why?"

"They don't know why! I asked them and they said they don't get paid to know why. Boy," cackled Tom, "I guess now the cars will have to slow down when they go past here. Wait till I tell Aunt Petal. This will get her up!"

It did, but this took a while. She had closed the door to her room and locked it. The work on the road was finished and the four-thirty whistle at the brick factory was blowing before she came, still in her nightshirt, to stand at a window with Tom and Kitty. The window did not command a good view of the lane or the road, but she said she could see all she wanted to see. "If having the bumps back will stop the cars from using the road as a raceway, we'll at least be that much to the good," she said. "No doubt this is some of Edwin's influence. I told him when he had the bumps taken out that it wasn't a good idea."

"It ruined our business," said Tom. "But now we're going to get it back."

Kitty left him and Aunt Petal there in the kitchen and went down the lane to where it connected with the road. The factory traffic was now out in full force. The astounded cars hit the bumps, and slowed, and went on. There was nothing for them to stop for. The road crew had removed the blackberry and marriage signs. Where they had been there were now only two bare posts bent a little to one side.

With a thoughtful finger to her lips Kitty stood looking at the posts. She was still looking at them when Edwin drove up. He was driving a new passenger car and took the bumps as carefully as one driving through a minefield. When he came abreast of the posts he pulled off to the side of the road, got out, turned, and walked back. Inspecting the bumps, bending toward them, he passed a booted foot over them.

Kitty hooked her thumbs in the pockets of her jeans and walked out to the road. When she was about four feet from Edwin she stopped, and as if picking up a piece of unfinished conversation, said, "They took the signs."

Taking his first notice of her, Edwin raised up and looked at her. "They were an eyesore."

Pleasantly Kitty said, "They were Aunt Petal's."

Unpleasantly Edwin said, "Well, I don't know where they are. Probably the men thought they were trash and dumped them somewhere."

"So somebody will have to find them and bring them back or else bring new ones," said Kitty.

Edwin's smile was ghastly. He stooped and began brushing sand from the toe of one of his boots.

Kitty started toward him. "If it hurts you to bend over, I'll do that for you. My back is younger than yours. Not much, but some."

Edwin straightened and jerked his foot away. "It doesn't hurt me to bend over. There is nothing wrong with my back."

"I was just going to brush the sand off your boot," protested Kitty.

"It's gone," said Edwin, "and I am too. I've got to get on home. We're going out for supper and Bauma doesn't like it when I drag in late."

Talking all the way, Kitty followed Edwin around to the driver's side of his car. "I thank you for having the bumps put back."

"Don't mention it," said Edwin, searching his pockets for his car keys.

"Some stepfathers aren't nice to their stepchildren, but you're nice to me and I thank you," said Kitty.

Edwin had the car door open but hadn't thought to look inside. Still looking for the lost keys, he transferred the contents of one pocket to another. "I said don't mention it."

"Tell Bauma I'm fine," said Kitty.

"I'll tell her," said Edwin and made another annoyed transfer.

"Most mothers worry about their children," said Kitty. "Especially when there's only one in the family."

Edwin pawed through a handful of change and loose keys. "Bauma is not worried about you. She knows you're getting all the care here you need."

"If I wasn't so busy with my own stuff, I'd go see her every day," said Kitty. "I can cook a little and I'd help her fix your supper so you'd have good things to eat when you got home. So you wouldn't have to go out. Do you like drop biscuits?"

"No," said Edwin.

"What about poor man's gravy?"

"No."

From where she was standing, Kitty could see the car keys dangling on a ring from the car's ignition switch. "Those are the only two things I know how to make. Bauma can't cook either. My father used to try and teach her, but she couldn't learn. When somebody is trying to teach somebody else how to cook, it should be a woman, shouldn't it?"

Edwin looked up from his pawing. "I suppose so." He spotted the lost keys, got into the car, and made as if to close its door, but couldn't because Kitty was in the way. She was standing with her back against the inside of the open door and didn't move except to lean toward Edwin. "Bauma told me that your mother knows how to cook."

"Please move," said Edwin. "I told you I've got to go."

"I think that's something," breathed Kitty. "And wouldn't it be something if she could come to visit you and teach Bauma how to do it? You could put a bed in your den and that could be her room."

Edwin pulled his seat belt up from its receptacle and tried to snap it over his round stomach, but it was tangled. He began the job of untangling it.

"If you and Bauma are going to go eat your supper in a fancy restaurant, why don't you invite me to go with you?" wheedled Kitty. "I wouldn't have to sit with you. I could sit at a table by myself."

"There aren't any fancy restaurants in Plainfield," said Edwin. He was still having trouble with the seat belt. He gave it a fierce jerk and it flew back into its hole.

"Well then, one of those places that sell hamburgers and french fries," urged Kitty. "Or one of those where you can get all the fried catfish and hush puppies you can eat for a dollar and ninety-nine cents."

Edwin spoke to the car's windshield. "Uhhh." He had given up on the seat belt. He started the car and again reached for its door.

This time Kitty took some steps backward, allowing Edwin to close the door. Until the dust, rising in the road, made a blur of it, she watched the car speeding homeward. She put a hand in her hair and chewed her lips. She wanted something. A change, an end to things, a new beginning, something. But a change, an end to things as they were, a new beginning, could not come. There was too much in between.

For their evening meal that day Kitty, Aunt Petal, and Tom ate boiled macaroni sprinkled with grated cheese. Aunt Petal had washed her hair, had bathed, and was fully dressed. She said it was the ague, gasping out its last breath, that had caused her to speak so foolishly earlier in the day about going to the old folks' home and selling Edwin her house and the woods.

Kitty brought the last of the watermelon from the icebox, and Aunt Petal said the rinds should be saved for making pickles. Before it grew dark she went out into the yard with Kitty and Tom to look at the wild garden and Tom's stylish horse. The horse, only begun, was covered with a damp cloth and lay under a cardboard box.

Kitty told Aunt Petal about the missing signs. "Edwin is going to either bring the old ones back or bring some new ones."

Aunt Petal had two comments. "Before he married Bauma he wouldn't have bothered to do either. Maybe his marriage is softening some of his old hard ways."

Chapter seven

Now that its head was her old hopeful self again, Aunt Petal's household settled back into routine. She took a sobering screwdriver to the washing machine, and when that didn't cure its drunken seizures and tantrums, knocked some sense into it with a hammer. After that it straightened up and behaved.

Aunt Petal and Kitty hung out a wash. Observing Kitty's clothes pinned to the line, Aunt Petal predicted that she would soon be walking around in a barrel if somebody didn't do something about her clothing situation. "Unless you're planning on joining a nudist colony you'd better go see Bauma and tell her you need some new clothes," she said.

"As soon as Edwin brings the signs back, I'll go," said Kitty. As long as her clothes were clean and covered her, they were, as they had always been, of little concern.

She learned how to make cornmeal mush, the grand kind that, when cold and sliced, comes from the griddle crisp and golden brown. Tom finished his stylish horse, or one that belonged behind a plow, and set it on a sunny window ledge to dry. Properly he had fastened its stub of a tail, its legs and ears to its chubby body with clay slip, the ceramist's glue. To make its short mane that lay on its neck in tendrils, he had forced clay through Aunt Petal's garlic press.

In the woods the blackberries were still abundant. The birds were ravenous for them and gobbled their share. It was time and past time for the summer rains, but so far there had been only one isolated shower. It swept in one night and hovered, clattering against the sides of the house and the roof. The roof of the sleeping porch sprung a leak and brought Aunt Petal with pots and pans to catch the leakage. In the woods all was still fresh and green, blazing green. "It's the minerals and air and water in the clay underneath that keeps it this way," gloated Aunt Petal.

She said nothing more about going to the old folks' home, but had plenty to say about the cost of sugar and glass jars. In exchange for a new supply of both she made some dresses for the woman who owned the country store. They had big pockets and took several days to make.

Each day Kitty watched and waited for Edwin to bring the signs, but he did not come and did not come. Early every morning and late every afternoon he passed Aunt Petal's place and slowed when he hit the bumps but did not stop or look anywhere except straight ahead.

Neither did Kitty's mother come or phone, and in harsh language Kitty nursed some strong thoughts. They are showing me what they think of me, she thought. They are telling me that I don't make any difference. Difference? Ha. I can make a difference and tomorrow I might just do it. Tomorrow as soon as Edwin gets home from work I might just go to his house and tell him all about Hubert. Then he and Ma will see how much difference I can make.

So ran Kitty's thoughts, but each time tomorrow came she would find an excuse not to go. She didn't know what it was that made her unwilling. It wasn't a lack of courage. She had courage.

She brought red pine lilies from the woods and set them out in the wild garden while Tom, working at his table under the tree, slapped and rolled clay, pinching it and pulling it into sausage-link shapes, this time for an elephant, next time for a cat.

Tom had questions. "The next time Mr. Edwin Johnson comes by here, why don't you run out and stop him and ask him when he's going to bring the signs back?"

"I might do it tomorrow," said Kitty.

"When are you going to tell him about the bricks you need for the playhouse?" inquired Tom.

"As soon as he brings the signs back," answered Kitty.

"When are you going to make your angel?" asked Tom.

"Maybe next week," said Kitty, dodging a definite answer because the angel was another thing that she kept putting off. Every time she thought of it and of telling Edwin about Hubert she would put her pillow over her face or hide behind something and laugh, but the laughs didn't sound like her voice. It was like somebody she didn't know was inside her making them. "I'll make the angel as soon as Edwin brings the signs back," she said.

Edwin did not bring the signs. He sent them with Shelley Ruth. Taking a short cut through the field just above Aunt Petal's house, she came one day right after the morning rush-hour traffic on Moon Lake Road had come and gone.

Kitty saw her coming and went out to meet

her. They met at the rock, the one with the lichens growing on its dark side. The sun had sent the last of the night dew away.

Shelley Ruth was carrying the old signs. Both were splintered as if by some tool with claws. "Mr. Johnson said for me to tell you that the men must have done it when they took them down," said Shelley Ruth. "He said if you wanted them fixed you should do it."

Kitty chalked up yet another mental black mark against Edwin. She held out her hands for the signs.

"I was supposed to take them on to your house," said Shelley Ruth. "It's on my way home. I have to go right past your house."

"You're going home now?" said Kitty. "But it isn't even noon yet."

Shelley Ruth handed over the signs. She wasn't in the least perturbed. "I don't have my job anymore. I got fired. Mr. Johnson's mother has come from Texas and I was in the way."

"Ahhhhh," said Kitty.

"So I get to go home," Shelley Ruth said, beaming. "Little Buster will be glad. He's Mama's youngest and screams when I leave him." Lingering, she had more to tell about Edwin's mother. "Her name is Violet and she cooks and sings. If you listen hard, maybe you can hear her from here."

The day was suddenly refreshed. Kitty faced

the Johnson house and stood in an attitude of listening. There was no sound in the meadow, not a hiss or a creak.

"Yesterday," confided Shelley Ruth, "she made tamale pie, and today she's making chili. I guess you can't hear her sing from here. It's too far away."

Kitty placed both signs on the rock. She didn't know how she would act or what she would say to Edwin's mother when she got to the Johnson house. She simply said a lucky goodbye to lucky Shelley Ruth and went, pausing now and then in the arid field to cock an expectant ear.

As she neared the house she could hear the singing, long, drawn-out notes that quivered and fell and gathered shorter ones and rose again to determined heights.

Happily appreciative, Kitty stood at the front door to the house for a couple of minutes. When no one answered her knocks she went around to the back door.

The kitchen singer was practicing what she sang, listening to the notes as they rolled from her mouth, pleased with their antics. She was a smaller version of Edwin, a pudgy female football player in a great apron, hovering over a great steaming pot. She was a mother in a son's kitchen, and the spicy red stuff simmering in her pot was her magic. She was Violet.

"But you're not to call me that," she said.

"And I don't want to be called Grandma either, because I'm not yours."

Kitty considered a solution. One way or another everybody was a cousin, so one more wouldn't hurt. "I could call you Cousin Violet when we see each other," she said, "but we won't be doing much of that, I think. I only come here when I need to see my mother about something. I make her nervous, and there are other reasons."

Kitty and Other Reasons were none of Cousin Violet's business. Her pure eyes said so. She had never made a mistake. Her pure eyes said that too. Every ten days she washed her hair in rainspout water and rinsed it with vinegar. Twice a year she went to a beauty shop for a permanent. As a younger woman she had had the good looks that go with plumpness. She still had a buttermilk complexion. As a girl she had been crowned queen of something—Watermelon Queen maybe.

Cousin Violet was tolerant only of the mistakes of others. These included Kitty. "Your mother," she said, "has a sick headache this morning. I don't wonder that she has. She and Edwin didn't get home last night till after midnight. They were out with friends. I haven't met any of their friends. They don't come here. For some reason Bauma doesn't ask them."

I am the reason, thought Kitty. You know about me, but the friends don't and if they came here you might let the old cat out of the old bag.

Cousin Violet had never slept between satin sheets. She didn't believe in them. In card games either. "Your mother went back to bed after Edwin left for work," she said. "She didn't eat when we did. If she'd put something in her stomach besides aspirin and water, she'd feel better. She ought to be out here learning how to cook. That's why I'm here. Edwin asked me to come and teach her, but I told him while we were having our breakfast that I was going home tomorrow. Your mother doesn't want to know how to cook."

"She might eat a bowl of your chili," said Kitty. "If you want me to, I'll take it in to her."

Cousin Violet said that in Texas people begged for her chili recipe, but when Kitty's mother lifted the napkin covering the bowl on the tray she fell back onto her pillow. "Chili. I can't stand it. The whole house smells of it, and I hate it. It's so common."

"It doesn't look common to me," said Kitty.

Her mother thumped out an aspirin tablet from the bottle on her nightstand, swallowed it dry, and sat up. A curl of steam rose from the bowl of chili.

"If you aren't going to eat it," said Kitty, "I will."

"Eat it," said her mother. "I can't. It makes me sick. Edwin thinks it's wonderful. He thinks his mother is wonderful. What did she say to you?"

Kitty ate a spoonful of the chili. It was pepper hot and delicious. "Not much. Naturally she doesn't want me to call her Grandma, so I'm going to call her Cousin Violet."

From the kitchen, through the closed bedroom door, there came a burst of song.

Kitty ate another spoonful of chili and a cracker. "I think she likes being Edwin's mother. I think when he was little she took him to Sunday school every Sunday so she could show him off. When you were married to Hubert he took me to Sunday school three or four times. I don't know if he did that to show me off."

Against her pillows her mother's hair stood out in a shiny brown mist. "Please don't spill any of that on my bed."

Kitty put the bowl of chili back on the tray and covered it with the napkin. "One time when Hubert took me to Sunday school it was raining when we got out. Now when it rains I think about him. The other night when it rained I did. But then I had to get up and help Aunt Petal put pots and pans around to catch the water. The roof to her sleeping porch leaks, and if we hadn't done that, I could have drowned."

"You tell Aunt Petal I said for her to either find another place for you to sleep or get her roof fixed," said her mother with a short show of authority.

"She can't get her roof fixed because she hasn't

got any extra money, and she can't find another place for me to sleep because she hasn't got any other rooms," said Kitty. "That's why I need some more bricks, so I can get my project built. So when it rains I can sleep in it."

Into her mother's face there came an uneasy look. "Bricks again. Well, how many more do you need for your project? What kind of a project is it?"

"It's going to be a playhouse and I don't know how many more bricks it will take," said Kitty. "Not any for the roof. I don't think the roof should be made out of bricks, but I don't know about that. I don't know about bricks. Men do. Edwin must. Hubert did. I remember when Hubert built his wishing well. He had only about six bricks left over when he got through."

Cannily her mother regarded her. "A brick playhouse."

"It isn't going to be very big," said Kitty. "One room. Under the big tree in Aunt Petal's side yard. I won't be afraid to sleep in it when it rains. At night I'll lock the door."

Her mother sat up and with her fingers rubbed her temples. Presently she got out of bed, padded over to the dresser, opened a drawer, withdrew an envelope, and came back to the bed with it. She had some terse news. "I've heard from your father. He isn't coming back to this state to live.

He's sold his house in Cottonville and has bought one in Colorado. He and his new wife and that kid he's adopted are going to live out there."

Kitty felt her breath leave her in a long sigh. My father, she thought, but after that the thought hung its head because, sigh as it might, memory could not now give again what it had given during the past two years—the shape of her father, the way he walked, his clothes. Those poor starved things had grown pale. They couldn't even whisper now. To believe again what she had believed that day before Brother had told her about Tildy was no longer possible. Her father didn't need her. He had a new wife. He had Tildy. He had Colorado.

Kitty felt her stranger's laugh coming and choked it off. A little of it came anyway, and her mother gave her a look. "He sent the money for the clothes you'll need for the next school term," Bauma went on. "He said he thought you'd need a new coat. Do you?"

"Yes," said Kitty. "My old one was too little and I gave it away."

Her mother offered the envelope. "The money is in here, but don't buy anything now. Wait till you go back to the Fords' and have one of them go with you to help pick out what you need."

"Did my father say I should go back to the Fords' to live?" asked Kitty.

"No, he didn't," said her mother. "But I've decided that's the best place for you."

"There won't be anybody there till the last week of August. Except whoever was going to come every day to feed the cat and make sure the house hasn't walked off."

"I know that. I called and was told."

"The cat's name is Gray Hunter," said Kitty. "Every day he brings Cook a present. A skink or a grasshopper."

"So you'll go as soon as the Fords get back," said her mother.

Kitty opened the envelope and looked at its contents, a sheaf of wrinkled currency.

"He sent cash," said her mother.

"I was looking for the letter," said Kitty.

"I threw it away," said her mother quickly, too quickly.

Kitty closed the envelope. It was white and long. There was no return address on it, no writing.

🔸 The singing coming from the kitchen hadn't stopped. The long notes slid around, wailing for something lost, and waited for the short ones to come in and help them out.

In her son's kitchen Cousin Violet was grimly enjoying herself. When she took the bedroom tray from Kitty she clucked her tongue and dumped the uneaten chili back into the pot.

Kitty went back through the meadow, stopping

at the rock long enough to pick up the signs. It was there that she wept, and wiped her eyes with her fists, and put the ache of weeping away. With no real knowledge of how she knew it, in a moment of terrible honesty, she spoke aloud to the empty pasture. "But I was never his anyway."

Chapter eight

O therwise busy with living, Aunt Petal looked at the injuries done to the signs, shrugged, and with wood putty and a small carpenter's saw repaired them.

Tom growled his disgust, dug into his boxes of art supplies, and produced paint and brushes. Kitty gave the signs new life by painting their whole surfaces black and painting new lettering—pink for the marriage sign and red for the blackberry. Aunt Petal said that Kitty should consider making sign painting her career.

"At school I'm always the one who gets to decorate the windows when it's Valentine's Day or Christmas," said Kitty. The glistening signs, attached again to their posts, satisfied the artist in her.

They did not impress Edwin. When he drove his truck into the yard the next afternoon at five o'clock he didn't mention them, although Kitty had watched him stop and look at them. He was alone and his truck was loaded with bricks. He said he would appreciate some help in unloading them.

"It will have to be me," said Kitty. "Aunt Petal and Tom went to town and aren't back yet. They went to see about getting the job of cleaning the Presbyterian manse. There isn't anybody living in it now, but as soon as the new minister comes there will be. Are you a Presbyterian or a Methodist?"

"Neither," said Edwin. "I'm a good Baptist." He slung his Texan's hat into the cab of the truck, pulled on his gloves, climbed up onto the back end of the truck, and began handing the bricks down to Kitty.

"They're for my playhouse," said Kitty. "And not only that, as soon as it's built I'll have a dry place to sleep when it rains. Aunt Petal's sleeping porch leaks."

Edwin was not gracefully parting with his

bricks. "You are an expensive person," he said.

"Yes," agreed Kitty, all cheer and friendliness. "But just think. If I have to come back here again, there will be a place all ready for me." She looked up and locked eyes with Edwin.

There was a thin glint in his. "I think you won't be coming here again."

With the flat of a hand, Kitty dusted a brick before setting it onto the growing pile. I think I won't either, she thought. I won't because Ma won't be here. Because soon now I'm going to make my angel and after that I'm going to tell you about Hubert and the annulment. Then Ma will have to take her satin sheets and go live with the horny lizards. She might have to eat them, poor lizards.

Edwin had come not only to deliver bricks but to say that which must have been festering in his mind since the day Kitty had come to Moon Lake Road. As a child will pick at a scab, he began to pick at the fester and sling pieces of it out to Kitty. "You shouldn't be here now. I don't know why you are."

"Because Mr. and Mrs. Ford went to Montana to see the Craggies and I didn't have anyplace else to go," said Kitty, as though explaining to a faulty memory.

"There are other places for children like you," said Edwin. "I don't know why Bauma didn't think to look into that before she sent you here to Aunt Petal's."

"It was that day you and Bauma got married," said Kitty. "Everybody was in a hurry, and Bauma didn't know what to do with me."

Edwin returned to the sore subject of his bricks. "These cost me plenty. They aren't the kind I give away. You don't need a playhouse, a big girl like you. Why do you need a playhouse? You'll be leaving here in August."

"Yes," said Kitty. "But the big rains will be here before then. Aunt Petal said when they come we'll all know it."

"It would be cheaper for me to send somebody to fix her roof," said Edwin.

"She wouldn't let you," said Kitty. "She won't let anybody do anything for her unless she can pay for it. She's got a whole list of things she can't pay for. She needs them but won't get them till she can pay for them."

Edwin had a retort. "Is she going to pay me for these bricks?"

Kitty laughed her own laugh. "No. Because they're not from you to her. They're from you to me."

"And they'll be here when you go," said Edwin churlishly. "But built into a playhouse. On Aunt Petal's property. Look here, did she put you up to this?"

"She doesn't know about the playhouse yet," said Kitty. "But she said Tom and I could make anything we wanted to out here."

"Look here," said Edwin. "I'm not crazy about any of this. I think I'm going to forget it and go on to my house and tell Bauma to start phoning."

"To find another place for me to stay till it's time for me to go?" said Kitty. "Yes," she said, gently speculating. "Maybe if Bauma phoned around, she could find another place for me. In town with some nice people. There must be some nice Mr. and Mrs. Somebody in town who would let me stay with them if she asked them. Or if you did. Everybody knows who you are. If you could find somebody else for me to stay with, maybe they wouldn't think it was strange. I would try to make them like me. They might not, though, because I talk a lot. About things that have happened to me."

Down to the last brick, Edwin stood holding it.

"So if you or Bauma could find another place for me to stay," said Kitty, "I wouldn't need the playhouse. You wouldn't have to send anybody to build it."

Above Edwin's head the branches of the oak tree hung full and still. A second, two seconds came and went. When they had gone Edwin handed down the last brick. "I see," he said. He did, too, but before he backed his truck out of Aunt Petal's yard he had a few more cryptic words. "You tell Aunt Petal I said that before I send somebody to build a playhouse out here I want her written permission. She can tape it to one of her signs and I'll pick it up tomorrow. I want it signed with her full legal name," ordered Edwin.

Out over the far reaches of the meadows and above Moon Lake the rays of the sun were the color of amber.

Kitty watered the plants in her garden and walked down the lane to where the signs were. Worrying a little that Tom and Aunt Petal were so late, she stood beside the signs watching the road for them.

They were late because the church member who had hired them to clean the Presbyterian manse had insisted that they start the job at once. Now they were in Chubby's Soda Shop tiredly celebrating, eating ice cream; chocolate for Aunt Petal and strawberry for Tom.

Crowded around a nearby table were other customers, four large boys who cracked their knuckles and thought of another joke to tell. Because kidhood still claimed them they were noisy. Because motherhood still claimed them they wore clean clothes and respectable hairstyles. They had sweet eyes, and when a girl in a green dress passed Chubby's window they sprawled against each other and made swooning sounds.

"They want us to look at them," said Aunt

Petal. "So don't. Eat your ice cream. Isn't it good? We'll take Kitty some. What flavor do you think she'd like?"

"Vanilla," said Tom. "But it would melt before we could get it home." He smelled of dried sweat. His hands were water-puckered. He had cleaned a fireplace as it had never been cleaned and had polished things that had forgotten about polish. The bathrooms had been the hardest; all that old soap scum, those little windows, all that chrome. On the chrome he had used a gallon of white vinegar and could still smell it. His ice cream tasted like it. He didn't want to hear what the boys at the next table were saying, but when one of them began to create a joke character named The Little Moron he sent a cold attentive look in that direction.

Chubby was outside sweeping the sidewalk in front of his shop. It didn't need sweeping, but Chubby needed the air.

"Tom," said Aunt Petal. "Finish your ice cream and we'll go."

With his spoon Tom made mush of his ice cream. Finished with hers, Aunt Petal took a pencil and notepad from her purse and started making a pay record for the church-member employer. "Let's see now. Each of us worked five-and-a-half hours today, didn't we?"

"Yes," said Tom. "Five-and-a-half."

"No," said Aunt Petal. "We took fifteen minutes off to rest, so that leaves five-and-a-quarter, not five-and-a-half."

"Five-and-a-quarter then," said Tom. He had his eyes riveted on the Little Moron's creator who had stood up, the better to be seen and heard. A talented entertainer, he made his wet mouth hang loose and crossed his vacant eyes. He shuffled his feet and flapped his arms. The Little Moron had a serious speech defect. He lisped his foolish words. Those seated at the table laughed.

"I don't think that's a bit funny," said Tom.

Aunt Petal put the pencil and notepad back in her purse. "Well, let's go before it gets worse." She spoke to someone she had never seen before, a boy cyclone who sprang from his chair.

It took three leaps for him to reach The Little Moron who was two heads taller than Tom, but Tom's arms and hands were strong. He grabbed The Little Moron by his shirtfront and hung on. "I said I don't think that's a bit funny! I don't think jokes about morons are funny!"

The Little Moron's creator didn't want to fight somebody younger and smaller than himself. Besides that, he knew that if he went home with a bloody nose or a torn shirt, his mother would put him to diving for pearls again. Pearl diving was what she called washing dishes, and every evening there were stacks of dirty ones. The Little

Moron's creator tried to free himself. "It was just a joke," he gasped. "I wasn't telling it to you. You didn't have to listen to it."

"I heard it and I didn't like it and I don't want you to tell it anymore," said Tom, and gave The Little Moron's creator such a hard shove that he staggered and wound up on the floor. The other boys at their table were embarrassed and looked away. They had stopped laughing.

Tom didn't waste any more time. He marched back to Aunt Petal and said, "Let's go."

Chubby was still outside sweeping the sidewalk. To Aunt Petal and Tom he said, "Come again." The streets of the town were peaceful.

On the way home Tom and Aunt Petal walked in silence, but after a while of that Aunt Petal pulled Tom's hand through the crook of her arm and patted it. "Tomorrow," she said, "we'll finish cleaning the manse. What are you going to do with your share of the money we earn?"

"Give it to whatever is next on our need list," said Tom. He had never been attracted much to bathtubs, but now he wanted a bath and he wanted supper. He forgot about both when he and Aunt Petal limped, footsore, into her side yard. For there under the oak was the stuff that was going to make Aunt Petal's prayer come true.

"More bricks," said Aunt Petal.

"Mr. Edwin Johnson must have brought them

to Kitty," said Tom, cuddling his excitement.

"But so many!" exclaimed Aunt Petal. "What is she going to do with so many?"

Tom's excitement didn't want to be cuddled. It wanted out, and along with Kitty's secret, Tom let it out. "She's going to build a playhouse!" he whooped. "And when she doesn't live here anymore it'll be your chapel!"

Aunt Petal sat on the ground and took off her shoes. On her way into the house she dropped one of them and didn't go back for it. In her room she removed her hat and gloves and put her pearl brooch back into its box. Before going to the kitchen, where Kitty was frying cornmeal mush for supper, she stood at her window for a long moment thinking about Edwin Johnson. And then not thinking about him. There were some things a person could not and should not question or think about, because once the questions and the thinking got started neither would stop.

Aunt Petal took off her soiled dress, put on a clean one, and went to the kitchen. At the sink she washed her clean hands. "When I told you and Tom that you could make anything in the side yard you want to make I didn't have anything in mind as grand as a brick playhouse," she said to Kitty.

"Edwin is going to send somebody to build it," said Kitty. "It will have a nice roof, so when the big rains come I'll have a dry place to sleep."

The mush slices in the pan were beginning to brown. Kitty turned them, and Aunt Petal set the table.

Tom had his bath before they ate, and afterward it was he who scampered down the lane to tape the signed permission paper to one of the signs. There was no wind that night, so it didn't blow away. The next morning, on her way to the Presbyterian manse with Aunt Petal and Tom, Kitty saw Edwin stop long enough to yank it off. She hadn't been hired to help finish cleaning the manse, but she worked that day as a paid employee would have.

The day after that the work on the playhouse started. The two men who came to build it said that they didn't need sidewalk superintendents, that they had forgotten more about brickwork than most people know. So Aunt Petal, Tom, and Kitty watched from the house.

Chapter nine

More accurately it was Tom and Aunt Petal who did most of the watching. Like small children at Christmas who want to know ahead of time what Santa is going to bring, they found excuses to make trips out into the yard. They said that the plants in the garden needed watering and that the branches needed to be picked up. They carried nice cold water in nice clean jars out to the bricklayers. Weren't the bricklayers thirsty?

"Yes," said the bricklayers. "But we brought

our own nice cold water in our own nice clean jars."

"We were wondering about the electricity," said Tom. "Kitty is going to sleep in the playhouse when it rains, and when it's dark she'll need to turn on the light."

"We don't know nothing about no electricity," said the bricklayers. "Go away."

Tom dared to assert himself. "It's our property. We've got a right to come out here and watch what you're doing. Go ahead with what you were doing. We aren't bothering you."

"You're bothering us," said the bricklayers, threatening to quit. So Tom and Aunt Petal sprinted back to the house to take up the watch from windows and doors. In a frenzy of activity Tom made some more clay animals—a dog, a hen, a rabbit, and a pig with a snout. But he had lost interest in making a likeness of his head. Making it would take too much of his valuable time, he said.

Aunt Petal cleaned cupboards, drawers, lampshades, and baseboards. She was a saver of string, buttons, pencil stubs, grocery bags, newspaper recipes, anything that might have a someday use. So what came out of the drawers and cupboards was studied and then either discarded or put back. The watermelon rinds intended for pickles had grown soggy. Aunt Petal threw them out. She cooked and sewed, but neither she nor Tom

118

could stay away from the windows and doors. They stood at the windows until they grew tired of standing. Then they took up their vigil in the doorway that opened out into the yard. Sitting close together in the open doorway, they watched the building of the playhouse. At noontimes they ate anything cold snatched from the icebox.

Aunt Petal's inner religion would not allow the question of electricity for the playhouse to be solved by anyone other than herself. "It won't need electricity until winter," she said. "Now it doesn't get dark till after we go to bed. We'll get the electricity before winter. Here. Let's just put it here on our need list. Ahead of everything else."

The need list hung on a string from a nail on the kitchen wall and was a foot long.

Some buyers of blackberry jam came. It was important that they be treated with unhurried courtesy and Aunt Petal and Tom did so. They smiled their best smiles. Tom held the labeled jars up to the light so the customers could see the prizes they were getting. Aunt Petal chatted about the weather, and from the sewing machine drawer Tom counted out the correct change into the waiting palms. But the instant the buyers had gone, the cupboard doors were closed with a bang and there was a gleeful race back to the doorway.

It was one of Tom's daily chores to empty the

ice-melt pan under the icebox. It filled and spilled over. Kitty emptied it and mopped up the puddle.

Now, except in the evenings when all in the yard was quiet, Kitty kept mostly to herself. Daytimes, when her mind was uncluttered, she didn't want the distraction of company, of talk. She wanted only to be left to herself, and under the windows in the sleeping porch made a place where she could work. Tom's table was the only one in the house tall enough for eye-level work, so she brought that in, placed one of the benches beside it, placed her tools and a good-sized package of clay on it.

With steady hands and a clear purpose in mind, Kitty cut away the clay's wrapper. This hour was going to mark the beginning of the end to things as they were.

The light streaming in through the windows caught the glints in her hair. She leaned toward the clay and spoke to it. "You," she said, "are going to be Hubert's angel."

It was a promise that wasn't kept all in one sitting, but presently the clay, mounted on a cylinder of clay serving as a neck, became a head with a face. There was a shy lift to its chin and in the corners of its mouth the suggestion of a coming smile. Its eyes were given lids, so that they appeared downcast. Instead of ears two egg-shaped clay rolls were pressed into the shape of wings.

To create hair Kitty used her comb and a modeling stick. She wasn't sure what kind of hair angels had, so gave hers ringlets. After the angel had dried a little, she scooped out a hole on top of its head and one in the side of its neck so that it would dry to the dryness of bone inside. She then pinched the hole openings together again with clay slip.

At night when the southern moon hung above the house and some sound would prod Kitty from sleep she would sit up in bed and gaze at the angel on the table under the window. And hold her pillow over her face to hide her stranger's laugh.

Her mother did not come, nor did she phone. Edwin did not come, nor did he slow as he passed Aunt Petal's place on his way to or from the brick factory.

By day the work on the playhouse went on. Some workers came with roofing, window, and flooring materials. They were friendlier than the bricklayers and swigged the water Aunt Petal and Tom took out to them. One of them took his wallet from his overalls pocket to show pictures of his grandchildren.

Along with Aunt Petal and Tom, Kitty looked at the pictures and ducked her head to see the one showing a baby with a toe in his mouth. Lucky baby, to be so loved, so wanted. Nobody would ever say he was somebody he wasn't. When he got old enough to have teeth and the front ones fell out, his mother wouldn't say how ugly he was. She would never put him in a room, lock the door, and go away with her friends. On his first day of school she wouldn't send him by himself. She would get out of bed and take him so he wouldn't be scared. Then she would go back to their house and clean all the rooms. She didn't play poker or any other kind of card game.

"The baby is a dear little fellow," Kitty told the grandfather.

"He's special," beamed the grandfather. It was he who put the lock on the playhouse door.

On the day after he and the other playhouse builders came and went for the last time, Kitty took her angel and Tom's animals to the brick factory.

Tom would not go with her. "The animals and your angel don't need to be baked," he said. "They're hard enough."

"They need to be fired," insisted Kitty. "Then we'll paint them and give them a coat of glaze so they'll be waterproof."

"It's going to rain," predicted Tom. "You'd better stay here and help me move your bed out to the playhouse."

"The man on the radio said it won't rain till day after tomorrow," said Kitty. "Help me put these boxes in the cart. No, don't touch the paper.

I wadded it up and stuffed it around like that to keep the pieces from rubbing against each other."

Tom lifted the boxes containing his animals and Kitty's angel and set them in the cart. Its wheels needed oiling and squealed as Kitty pulled it down the lane to the road, but its cargo was well packed and didn't shift. Around it and over it Kitty had spread sheets of newspaper, fastening them to the cart's railing with pinch clothespins.

Tom skipped alongside but went only as far as the signs. Because of the playhouse he now grudgingly saw some good in Edwin. Yet he still remembered the humiliation of going to the factory to ask for free bricks and being turned away. He had more predictions. "It's got a guard at the gate and he won't let you in."

"He'll let me in when I tell him I'm Edwin's cousin," said Kitty. It was then about nine o'clock.

At twenty minutes or so past nine Kitty stood at the gate to the brick factory trying to persuade its guard to open it. "I am Mr. Johnson's cousin and I've got to see him about something."

The guard was a simple man. He adored his boss and his eventless job. He knew both. Also he knew mischief when he saw it. "Mr. Johnson don't have any cousin in Plainfield," he said. "He's from Texas."

"I am Mrs. Johnson's cousin," said Kitty. "So that makes me Mr. Johnson's cousin too."

"Honey," said the guard, "why are you coming here telling me that story? If you was Mrs. Johnson's cousin, you'd know that she's gone with Mr. Johnson to a brickmakers' convention. Why don't you go on now? This here is a legitimate place of business. We don't have time to play games."

"I am not playing a game," said Kitty. "I am here on business."

"Tell me what it is," said the guard. "What you got there all covered up in your cart?"

"Some animals and an angel," said Kitty. "I want to bake them in one of Edwin's kilns."

The guard stepped back. Through the gate's heavy wire meshing he looked at Kitty. "Honey, this here is a brick factory. We don't bake animals and angels. We bake bricks. You'd better go on back home now. Somebody is probably wondering where you are."

Defeated, Kitty turned the cart around. The paper covering the animals and the angel had worked its way loose of one of the clothespins. She bent to refasten it. She thought of Yellow Hair and turned back to the guard. Did he know Yellow Hair?

"That's her name?" said the guard. "Yellow Hair?"

"Cousin Edwin's assistant," said Kitty. "She knows who I am. Could you ask her to come out here?"

The guard went to the guard hut standing just inside the gate and phoned Yellow Hair, who came at once from her office. Efficiently she solved everything. Yes, certainly the animals and the angel could be fired in one of the factory's kilns. She, Yellow Hair, knew just the man for the job. He would know at what temperature and for how long the pieces should be baked. Possibly this would take about six hours. Could Kitty come back after the pieces tomorrow? They would surely be ready by then.

"I will be back tomorrow," said Kitty. And wheeled the empty cart back to Aunt Petal's. She and Tom moved her bed from the sleeping porch to the playhouse. That night she slept in it. The door was locked and she was dry and safe.

The rain held off, but the promise of it was all around, so Tom and Kitty brought firewood from the woods and stacked it against the wall on the back porch.

Kitty went back to the factory for the animals and the angel. Their hours in the kiln had turned them bright red. Tom let his horse, his dog, and his hen stay that color because it was right for them, but with water paints made the pig pink and the rabbit pink and white. Kitty painted her angel white except for its wings and hair. She painted its wings palest blue and its hair yellow. All of the animals and the angel were then given a coat of clear glaze. Then Kitty took them back to the factory to be fired again.

The rain came, but at first all it did was play. Some big drops splashed here and some there. A trace fell on the woods and on the meadow above Aunt Petal's house. The air smelled of heat and dust.

Edwin and Kitty's mother came. From the door opening out into Aunt Petal's yard Kitty watched them drive in. They looked at the playhouse but didn't get out of the car. Motioning to Kitty from his window, Edwin waved a piece of paper.

It had begun to mist. The air was heavy with it. Through the mist Kitty walked out to the car and stood on the driver's side of it. Grinning, she said, "See the playhouse? They got it built."

"I hope I've heard the last of it," said Edwin.

"Aren't you going to get out and look at it?" said Kitty.

To see around Edwin, Kitty's mother had to lean forward. "We'll come tomorrow to see it. We're just back from a convention and in a hurry to get home."

Offering the piece of paper, Edwin stuck his hand out the window. "It's a check for Aunt Petal. Please give it to her."

"You want to give it to her yourself?" said Kitty. "No, wait. You can't. She and Tom went to town to see about another job and aren't back yet."

"Give her the check when she gets back," said Edwin.

"I thought you came to see the playhouse," said Kitty.

"No," said her mother. "We only stopped to leave the check. Tell Aunt Petal I'm sorry to be late with it. I forgot it and didn't think of it until this morning. That's all we stopped for. We've been driving since noon and we're tired."

Today Edwin was not a loving husband. He took his necktie off and threw it into the backseat. In an unloving tone he said, "I have been driving since noon. You slept most of the way."

"I had a headache," said Kitty's mother.

"You've always got a headache," said Edwin. "You wouldn't have if you'd eat like I do. Why can't you? It wouldn't hurt you to gain a couple of pounds."

"Can we go?" said Kitty's mother.

"Yes," said Edwin politely, too politely. He would have started the car and backed it out of the yard if Kitty had not stopped him. "Don't go yet," she said. "You can't go till I give you your present. I made it for both of you and I want you to have it. It's in the playhouse and I'll run get it if you'll sit here a minute."

"We'll get it tomorrow," said her mother. "I've been cooped up here in this car for five hours and want to get home. We'll come back tomorrow and get the present."

If I have to, I'll throw myself down in front of the car and to get out of here they'll have to run over me, thought Kitty. I can only do this once and it's got to be now. "But I want you to have it today," she said.

"Edwin," said her mother, "I said I want to get on home."

"Bauma," said Edwin. "Shut up. Just shut up. It's always what you want. Why can't you ever think that sometimes I want too, and right now I do. I want the present. Today." He didn't look like somebody who wanted a present. He looked like somebody spoiling for a fight. In an ugly voice he said to Kitty, "Go get the present."

Great day, great hour. It had come, this great delicious hour.

The mist on Kitty's head and bare arms was chill. Under her bare feet the grass was slick.

The inside of the playhouse was cozy warm. Its closed windows were fogged over, were peppered with fine mist, but by the time Kitty emerged from it the mist was no longer that. It had turned into rain. Long streamers of rain came weaving out of the woods and from all directions. It was light and eerie. In the yard it fell straight down. There was no sound to it.

In the yard, in the car, Edwin and Kitty's mother sat waiting for the present. The window on Edwin's side of the car was still down.

In the rain Kitty crossed the yard to the car. She was calm as she handed the angel in to Edwin. So that what she had to say wouldn't be lost on her mother, she stood as close to the car door as she could get and inclined her head. "I got the idea for it from a man I know."

With both hands Edwin held the angel. He was scornfully amused. "But it's only a clay model of a child's head. Ordinary. I've seen dozens like it. Ordinary except for its ears. Why are its ears wings instead of ears?"

"It's not just a clay model of a child's head," said Kitty, ever so gently. "Don't you see what it is? It's an angel. A man I know had one. He carried it around on his shoulder. It talked to him and he talked to it. It wasn't real, but he thought it was."

Edwin turned and handed the angel to Kitty's mother. "Here's our present."

"And there's lots more I've got to tell you about that man," said Kitty, looking straight into her mother's eyes.

A watered wind blew across Moon Lake and then across Moon Lake Road. It made the rain streamers slant, and wanting to drag out what she had to say, Kitty shifted her gaze from her mother's frozen face to what lay beyond it. Water dripped from the end of her nose. Her hair was plastered with water.

Beyond the closed window on the passenger's side of the car the playhouse looked like a little church waiting for its congregation to come and sing holy songs. And bow their heads and pray to be delivered of their sins.

Kitty brought her gaze back and rested it on her mother's still face. She thought she would laugh or scream or howl. She did none of those things. "That man's name," she said. "That man's name." And there her voice stopped. She couldn't go on because from some source of gentility and breeding, from some alien well of refinement and intelligence there rose in her something that stepped in and took hold. It had a heart and the heart of it was hopeful. It was willful and wouldn't let go. It beat a command, saying, "Hear me! Hear me! Hear me!"

Under the attack of this, Kitty licked her trembling lips and stood on first one foot and then the other. The beating in her did not stop. "That man's name," she said. "Well, I can't remember his name. Anyway, he was sick. He's dead now, somebody told me."

Disgusted, Edwin said, "Uhhhh," and started the car.

Still holding the angel, Kitty's mother sat back in her seat. To Edwin she said, "You'd better roll up your window."

130

Kitty stood back from the car and watched it leave the yard. The plants in her wild garden were guzzling the rain, rejoicing in it. Snuggled among their leaves and stems, Tom's animals looked out. The air now was clean.

Great hour. It was still a great hour, greater still than it had started out to be, for in it there was a sense of completion.

Kitty had started to heal.

Chapter
ten

She was the first of the Fords' paying guests to report in come the last week in August. From the bus station she took the town's only taxi. Its driver was the same one who had taken her to the bus station in June, so she sat in the front seat with him. As they rattled along through the old cobbled streets they talked.

"I thought I had seen the last of you in June," said the driver.

"Sometimes I fool people," said Kitty.

"What did you do with your summer?" asked the driver.

"I made an angel," replied Kitty.

The taxi driver was used to remarks that didn't make sense, especially from kids. Half of the time he didn't understand what his own kids were talking about. He had never studied any of the writings of the old Greek philosophers. He didn't know where Greece was, but he was convinced his three-year-old could speak the language of that country. The kid and the Greek who owned the Eldorado Café never had any trouble understanding each other. The Greek didn't speak much American.

"One of my boys says things like you just said," commented the driver. "We think he's going to be a scientist."

"That takes intelligence," said Kitty.

"My other boys are going to be millionaires," said the driver. "They don't know how they're going to do it, though. We tell them to be satisfied if they can be thousandaires."

"I don't know what I'm going to be," said Kitty. "Something that will use my intelligence." Eager to share her new, attractive, and comforting belief, she said, "I think I must have got my intelligence from my father." She hadn't thought about the taxi driver once all summer, so now it was strange to realize that she had been homesick for him.

She found out too just how homesick she had been for Mr. and Mrs. Ford, for the cat Gray Hunter, for the familiar room at the top of the stairs, and for Cook, who never let anybody get away with anything.

"Eat that sandwich," ordered Cook. "It'll dry out if it's saved."

The sandwich was a thick slab of warm meat loaf stuffed into a long roll.

Cook took raisin pies from the oven and sat down to rest. The cat came to rub his head against her feet. She set him in her lap. "I got your letter. The reason you didn't get an answer is because after I wrote it I stuck it in my purse and it got buried under all the other stuff I carry around. When I was looking for a paper clip yesterday I found it. You want it?"

"What does it say?"

"Nothing. It's all about the family reunion."

"Did everybody fight?"

"Sure. We had a fighting good time."

"I was going to fight with my mother. But I changed my mind. I don't hate her anymore."

"I never knew you did," said Cook.

"Because she's my mother," said Kitty simply.

"Eat your sandwich," said Cook. The cat reached up to put a paw on her cheek. She set him on the floor, and he bounded to the door and stood there waiting to be let out. The skinks and grasshoppers weren't so plentiful now, but for him outside was better than inside except when it was food time or lap time or sleep time. At sleep time he knew where he was welcome. He shared Kitty's pillow or the foot of her bed, whichever was the more convenient for him.

In Kitty's letters to Tom and Aunt Petal she wrote about Gray Hunter.

In one of Tom's return letters he said he thought he might get Aunt Petal a cat like Gray Hunter, a brindle. He spelled brindle wrong so that it came out *brindler*.

The first frost didn't come until the week before Christmas. Then the ground was white with it, and all day it didn't melt. Mr. Ford kept a crackling fire going in the living room fireplace.

School let out for the holiday and some of the girls went home for it. Those that didn't helped Mrs. Ford put up the big tree in the hall and cracked nuts for Cook's fruitcakes.

Kitty made a wreath of holly and red ribbon to hang on the front door.